Joseph Rawson Lumby

Be domes dæge, - de die judicii

An Old English version of the Latin poem ascribed to Bede

Joseph Rawson Lumby

Be domes dæge, - de die judicii
An Old English version of the Latin poem ascribed to Bede

ISBN/EAN: 9783744714938

Printed in Europe, USA, Canada, Australia, Japan

Cover: Foto ©Andreas Hilbeck / pixelio.de

More available books at **www.hansebooks.com**

Be Domes Dæge,

De Die Judicii,

AN OLD ENGLISH VERSION OF THE LATIN POEM ASCRIBED TO BEDE.

EDITED (WITH OTHER SHORT POEMS) FROM THE UNIQUE MS. IN THE
LIBRARY OF CORPUS CHRISTI COLLEGE, CAMBRIDGE,

BY

J. RAWSON LUMBY, B.D.,

FELLOW OF ST. CATHERINE'S COLLEGE, AND FORMERLY FELLOW OF MAGDALENE COLLEGE,
CAMBRIDGE.

LONDON :

PUBLISHED FOR THE EARLY ENGLISH TEXT SOCIETY, BY
N. TRÜBNER & CO., 57 & 59, LUDGATE HILL.

MDCCCLXXVI.

PREFACE.

THE poems contained in this volume form part of a MS. in the Library of Corpus Christi College, Cambridge, now numbered CCI., but marked in the old Catalogue and in Wanley as S.18. The portion of the MS. here printed commences at page 161, and is written in a different hand from that part of the volume which precedes it. A complete list of the contents of this valuable MS. is given in Wanley's Catalogue, pp. 137 seqq., and need not be repeated.

The first two pieces here printed have never been put forth before, with the exception of the few lines given in Wanley, some of which were copied into Conybeare's Illustrations of Anglo-Saxon Poetry (p. lxxx of the introductory Catalogue), but with the mistakes which are in Wanley exactly repeated. Prof. Conybeare had evidently never seen the MS., or he would have given the lines as they are now printed.

In sending forth these texts the sole aim of the Editor has been to put into the reader's hands as complete a representation of the words of the MS. as a printed text can furnish. Either in the text or in the margin the reader will find every letter of the original supplied to him.

Very few notes have been added, but a copious index verborum is appended. This seemed likely to be of more service than notes.

The first of these five poems is an Old English version of what is variously represented as Bede's, or as Alcuin's Latin poem, "De Die Judicii." The Latin text which is herewith printed is taken from the collection of writings attributed to

Bede, and appended to the genuine works of that father published in Migne's Patrologia. But a large portion of the same poem will be found among the works ascribed to Alcuin. In Frobenius' edition of Alcuin, 1777, it is given, with sixteen lines of introduction, at page 616, vol. iii., among the Addenda et Supplenda. The Old English version is of course much later than the date of either of these writers.

The second poem, which the editor has entitled Lár, follows in the MS. immediately after the first, and appears to be an exhortation designed to supplement the former poem.

Wanley has printed the other three poems *in extenso*, and they have been published by Grein among the specimens in his Bibliothek. A few errors which occur in Wanley, and which in some places Grein has emended conjecturally, have been corrected in the present reprint of the poems, and to the whole a rendering in modern English, as literal as was possible, has been supplied.

It will be seen that the poems are defective in many places, as shown by the faulty alliteration in some lines, and here and there by the absence of half a line or more at a time, especially in that curious medley, the Oratio Poetica. The Editor leaves to others the labour of conjectural emendations. He has to thank many friends for suggestions while the sheets have been going through the press, and the authorities of Corpus Christi College for the kindness with which they arranged that he might have access to the MS. To one of their number, the Rev. W. M. Snell, he is also indebted for a careful final reading of the printed text with the MS.

CAMBRIDGE,
Feby. 1876.

CONTENTS.

Be Domes Dæge.

INCIPIUNT VERSUS BEDÆ PRESBYTERI.

De Die Judicii.

Inter florigeras fecundi cæspitis herbas
Flamine ventorum resonantibus undique ramis, etc.

Hwæt ic ana sæt innan bearwe
mid helme beþeht· holte tomiddes·
þær þa wæterburnan swegdon and urnon
4 on middan gehæge· eal swa ic secge·
eac þær wynwyrta· weoxon and bleowon
innon þam gemonge on ænlicum wonge·
and þa wudu-beamas wagedon and swegdon·
8 þurh winda gryre· wolcn wæs gehrered·
and min earme mod eal wæs gedrefed·
þa ic færinga· forht and unrot·
þaſ unhýrlican fers· onhéfde mid sange·
12 eall ſwylce þu cwæde· synna gemunde·
lifes leahtra· and þa langan tid·
þæs dimman cyme· deaðes on eorðan ;
Ic ondræde me eac· dom þone miclan·
16 for mandædum· mínum on eorðan·
and ꝥ éce ic éac· yrre ondræde me·
and synfulra gehwam· æt sylfum gode·
and hu mihtig frea· eall manna cynn·
20 todæleð and todemeð· þurh his dihlan miht ;
Ic gemunde eac· mærðe drihtnes·
and þara haligra on heofonan rice·
swylce earmsceapenra· yfel[1] and witu ;

[1] MS. yfeſ.

OF DOOMSDAY.

Lo! I lonely sat within a bower,
With shade bedecked, amidst a wood,
Where the water-burns murmured and ran,
4 Amid an inclosure, all as I say.
There also pleasant plants waxed and bloomed,
Amid the gathering in a peerless meadow ;
And the trees of the wood waved and rustled,
8 Through roaring of the winds the welkin was desolated,
And my sad mind was all troubled.   my mind was troubled
Then I suddenly, fearful and sad,
This gloomy verse began to sing,
12 All such as thou mayest speak of, mindful of sins,   at my sins,
Of the faults of life, and the long tide
Of the coming of dark death on earth.   and the coming of death.
I trembled for myself eke at that great doom,
16 For my sinful deeds upon earth.
And I likewise trembled for myself at that eternal ire,   I trembled at
And for each sinful one from God himself,
And how the mighty Lord, all men's kin
20 Will sever and doom through his secret might.   God's doom, and thought of the blessed and the cursed.
I minded me eke of the glory of the Lord,
And of those holy-ones in heaven's kingdom :
Likewise of the wretched, their evil and punishment.

24 Ic gemunde þis mid me· and ic mearn swiðe·
and ic murcnigende cwæð· mode gedrefed ;
Nu ic eow æddran· ealle bidde·
ꝥ ge wylspringas· wel ontynan·

¹ MS. os.

28 hate on¹ hleorum· recene to tearum·
þænne ic synful slea ſwiðe mid fyſte·
breost mine beate· on gebed stowe·
and minne lichaman lecge on eorðan·

32 and gearnade sar ealle ic gecige·
Ic bidde eow benum nuða·
ꝥ ge ne wandian· wiht for tearum·
ac dreorige hleor· dreccað mid wope·

36 and sealtum dropum sona ofer geotaþ·
and geópeniað mán· ecum drihtne·
Ne þær owiht inne ne belife
on heort-scræfe· heanra gylta·

40 ꝥ hit ne sy dægcuð· ꝥ ꝥ dihle wæs·
openum wordum· eall abæred·
breoſtes· and tungan· and flæsces swa some·
Ðis is an hæl· earmre sauwle·

44 and þam sorgiendum· seleſt hihta·

² MS. wopa.

ꝥ he wunda her wope² gecyðe·
uplicum læce· Se ana mæg.

³ MS. aglidene
gyltas· mod-
god gode ge-
hælan.

agiltende gyltas· mid gode gehælan·³

48 and ræplingaſ recene onbindan·
ne mid swiðran his swyþe nele brysan·
wanhydig gemod wealdend engla·
ne þone wlacan smocan· waces flæſceſ·

52 wyle waldend criſt· wætere gedwæscan·
Hu ne gescéop þe se scaþa· scearplice bysne·
þe mid criste wæs· cwylmed on rode·
hu micel forstent· and hu mære is·

56 ſeo so e hreow· synna and gylta·
se sceaða wæs on rode· ſcyldig and manful·
mid undædum· eall gesymed·

24 I minded this with myself, and I mourned greatly,
And murmuring I spake, troubled in mind.
Now, ye veins, I bid you all
That ye open well the wellsprings

I bade my
tears fall ;

28 Hot on my face quickly for tears.
Then I, sinful, strike strongly with fist,
Beat my breasts in the place of prayer ;
And my body I lay on the earth,

I beat my breasts,
and lay on the
earth.

32 And as deserved I invoke all pains.
I bid you now with prayers
That ye slack not at all for tears ;
But dreary face vex ye with weeping,

I bid you all

36 And with salt drops soon overshed,
And open your sin to the Eternal Lord.
Let there no whit remain within,
In heart cave, of grievous guilts,

40 So that it be not day-clear that which was secret,
With open words all laid bare,
Of breast and tongue and flesh also.
This is only salvation of a poor soul,

confess your sins
to God,

44 And to the sorrowful best of hopes :
That he his wounds here by weeping make known
To the leech on high. He only may
The offenders in guilt with good heal,

that he may heal
you.

48 And the prisoners quickly unbind,
He truly will not bruise with his right hand
Thoughtless heart, ruler of angels :
Nor the faint smoke of weak flesh

He will not
bruise you.

52 Will Christ the ruler with water quench.
Did not the thief warn thee sharply with example,
Who with Christ was slain on the cross,
How much avails, and how grand is,

Think how the
thief on the
cross

56 That true sorrow for sins and offences ?
The thief was on the cross, guilty and sinful,
With wrongdoings all laden :

he drihtene swa þeah· deaðe gehende·
60 his bena bebead· breoſtgehigdum·
   he mid lyt wordum· ac geleaffullum·
   his hæle begeat· and help recene
   and in-gefor· þa ænlican geatu·
64 neorxnawonges· mid nerigende·
   Ic acsige þé la earme geþanc·
   hwi lataſt þu ſwa lange· ꝥ þu ðe læce   ne

cyþst·¹

   oððe hwi ſwigaſt þu· synnigu tunge·
68 nu þu forgifnesse hæfst· gearugne timan·
   nu þe ælmihtig· earum atihtum·
   heofonrices weard· gehyreð mid luſtum·
   Ac se dæg cymeð· ðonne demeð god·
72 eorðan ymbhwyrft þu ana scealt·
   gyldan scad wordum· wið scyppend god·
   and þam rican frean· riht agyldan·
   Ic lære ꝥ þu beo hrædra· mid hreowlicum tearum·
76 and ꝥ yrre forfoh· eces deman·
   hwæt ligſt þu on horwe· leahtrum afylled·
   flæsc mid synnum· hwi ne feormast þu·
   mid teara gyte· torne synne·
80 hwi ne bidst þu þe beþunga and plaſter·
   lifes læcedomes· æt lifes frean·
   nu þu scealt greotan tearas geotan·
   þa hwile tima sy· and tid wopes·
84 nu is halwende· þæt man her wepe·
   and dædbote do· drihtne to willan·
   Glæd bið se godes sunu· gif þu gnorn þrowast·
   and þe sylfum demſt· for synnum on eorðan·
88 ne heofenes god· henða and gyltas·
   ofer ænne syþ wrecan wile ænigum men ;
   Ne scealt þu forhyccan· heaf and wopas·
   and forgifnesse· gearugne timan·
92 gemyne eac on mode· hu micel is ꝥ wite·

He to the Lord, nevertheless, nigh unto death,
60 His prayer bade with heart-thoughts :
He with few words, but full of faith,
His salvation obtained, and help speedily,
And fared in at the peerless gates
64 Of Paradise, with the Redeemer.
I ask thee, O poor mind,
Why lingerest thou so long, that thou showest not thy-
self to the leech ?
Or why art thou silent, sinful tongue,
68 Now thou for forgiveness hast ready time ?
Now thee, the Almighty, with attentive ears,
Ward of heaven's kingdom, will hear with pleasure ;
But the day cometh when God will doom
72 The circuit of earth. Thou by thyself shalt
Give account with words to God the Creator,
And to the mighty Lord rightly account.
I rede thee that thou be beforehand with penitent tears,
76 And that anger prevent of the Eternal Judge.
Why liest thou in dust with offences filled,
O Flesh ! with sins ? Why dost thou not cleanse away,
With flood of tears, grievous sins ?
80 Why askest thou not for thyself bathings and plaster,
Life's leechdoms, of life's Lord ?
Now shouldst thou greet, tears pour forth,
While time is, and weeping-tide.
84 Now is it beneficial that man here weep,
And penance do at the Lord's will.
Glad is the Son of God if thou sorrow bearest,
And thyself judgest for sins on earth.
88 Ne'er heaven's God wrongs and guilts
Above one time will wreak on any man ;
Nor shouldst thou despise wailing and weeping,
And of forgiveness the ready time.
92 Think also in soul how great is the punishment,

Marginal notes:
by prayer gat help,

and went to Paradise.

Why dost not thou ask forgive-ness now!

Why dost thou not cleanse thy sins with thy tears!

Glad will Christ be of thy sorrow.

þe þara earmra byð· for ærdædum·

oþþe hu¹ egeſlic· and hu andrysne·

heah-þrymme cyninge· her wile deman·

96 anra gehwylcum be ærdædum ;

Oþþe hwylce forebeacn· feran onginnað·

and criſtes cyme cyþað on eorðan ;

Eall eorðe bifað· eac swa þa duna

100 dreosað and hreosað·

and beorga hlida bugað and myltað.

² MS. sǽ.
and se egeslica sweg· ungerydre sǽs²

eall manna mod· miclum gedrefeð

104 eal bið eac upheofon·

³ MS. geþux-
sað.
sweart and gesworcen· swiðe gewuxsað·³

deorc and dim hiw· and dwolma sweart·

þonne stedelease steorran hreosað·

108 and seo sunne forswyrcð· sona on morgen·

ne se mona næfð nanre mihte wiht·

ꝥ he þære nihte genipu mæge fleogan·

eac þonne cumað hider· ufon of heofone

112 deað beacnigende· bregað þa earman ;

þonne cumað upplice· eored-heapas

ſtiþ-mægen astyred· styllað embútan·

eal engla werod ecne behlænað ;

116 Ðone mæran metod· mihte and þrymme ;

Sitt þonne sigel-beorht· swegles brytta·

on heah setle· helme beweorðod ;

We beoð færinga· him beforan brohte·

120 æghwanum cumene· to his ansyne·

That gehwilc underfó dom be his dædum· æt drihtne
sylfum ;

Ic bidde man that þu gemune· hu micel bið se
broga

beforan domsetle drihtneſ þænne·

124 stent he heortleas· and earh·

amasod· and amarod· mihtleas· afæred·

That to the wretched shall be for former sins.
Either how aweful and how dreadful
A King in his majesty here will judge

Think of God's
Judgement Day,

96 Each man by his former deeds.
Or what tokens begin to fare,
And Christ's coming show on earth.

and the tokens
that come be-
fore it.

Earth all shaketh, and likewise the mountains
100 Perish and fall,
And the doors of the graves bend and melt;

The graves shall
open,

And the fearful noise of the boisterous sea
All men's hearts much affrighteth,
104 Utterly also is heaven above
Swart and cloudy, quickly it waxeth
Dark and dim-hued, and a swart chaos.
Then stedless stars fall,

the stars shall
fall.

108 And the sun grows dark early in the day,
Nor has the moon aught of any might
That she the night's clouds may disperse.
Also then shall come hither, down from heaven,
112 Death-tokenings, affright the miserable:
Then shall come on high mighty hosts,
A strong power stirred they hurry around.
The hosts of all angels surround the Eternal

Then, with hosts
of angels, shall
God come,

116 The great Creator, with might and host.
There shall sit, sun-bright, the firmament's ruler
On high throne with crown honoured,
We shall be suddenly brought before him,

and we shall

120 From all sides coming to his presence;
That each may receive doom for his deeds from the be doomed.
　　Lord himself.
I bid, O man, that thou remember how great will
　　be the terror
Before the Lord's judgment-seat then.
124 He stands heartless and timorous,
Amazed and disturbed, powerless, terrified;

þænne samod becumað· of swegles¹ hleo·
eall eugla werod· ecne ymtrymmað.

128 æne bið geban micel· and aboden þider·

eal adames cnosl· eorðbuendra²
þe on foldan wearð· fedend æfre·
oððe modar gebær· to manlican·

132 oþþe þa þe wæron· oððe woldon beon·

· oþþe to-wearde· geteald wæron awiht ;
Ðonne eallum beoð ealra gesweotolude·
digle geþancas· on þære dægtide·

136 eal ꝥ seo heorte· hearmef geþohte·
oððe seo tunge to teonan geclypede·
oþþe mannes hand· manes gefremede·
on þystrum scræfum· þinga on eorðan·

140 eal ꝥ hwæne sceamode· scylda on worulde.
ꝥ he ænigum men. ypte. oððe cyðde ;
þonne bið eallum open· æt somne
gelíce· alyfed ꝥ man lange hæl ;

144 Ufenan eall þis eac byð gefylled
eal uplic lyft· ættrenum lige·
færð fýr ofer eall· ne byð þær nan foresteal·
ne him man nane mæg miht forwyrnan ;

148 eal³ ꝥ us þincð æmtig eac⁴ gemearces·
under roderes ryne· readum lige
bið emnes mid þy· eal gefylled ;
Ðonne fyren líg blawað and braslað.

152 read and reaðe· ræsct and efesteð·
hu he synfullum susle gefremede·
Ne se wrecenda brynæ· wile forbugan·
oððe ænigum þær· are gefremman·

156 buton he horwum sy· her afeormad·
and þonne þider cume· þearle aclænsad ;
þonne fela mægða· folca unrim
heora sinnigan breost· swiðlice beatað·

160 forhte mid fyste· for fyren-lustum ;

Then together will come from the firmament's shade
All the hosts of angels, the Eternal surround.
128 At once will be a loud proclamation, and called thither
All Adam's race, of earth inhabitants,   All Adam's race
shall appear,
That on earth have been supported ever,
Or mother bare in human form,
132 Or those that were or should be,
Or who were at all about to be reckoned.
Then to all will be of all disclosed   all secrets shall
be known,
The secret thoughts, on the day-tide,
136 All that the heart of harm devised,
Or the tongue for injustice spake,
Or man's hand of evil framed,
In dark caves, of things on earth;
140 All that any one shamed of sins in the world   and all shames.
That he to any man should open or tell,
Then will be to all open altogether,
Alike set free that man long hid.
144 Beside all this, also will be filled
All the lofty lift with poisonous fire.
Fire will fare over all, nor will be there any hindrance: Fire will be over
all,
Nor himself by any means may man forewarn.
148 All that we think empty also of boundary,
Under the roaring of the sky with red blaze,
Will be all alike therewith utterly filled.
Then the flame of the fire will blow and crackle,
152 Red and angry, will rush and hurry
How it for the sinful torture might prepare.   and torture all
Nor will the punishing flame forbear,
Or towards any there act with favour;
156 Unless he be here from filth cleansed,   who are not
cleansed from
And then thither come throughly clean.   sin.
Then many races, of folks without number,
Their sinful breasts strongly will beat,
160 Fiercely with fist, for their gross luxury.

þær beoð þearfan and þeod-cyningas·
earm and eadig ealle beoð afæred·
þær hæfð ane lage earm and se welega.
164 forðon hi habbað ege· ealle ætsomne;
Dæt reðe flod ræscet fyre·
and biterlice bærnð· ða earman saula·
and heora heortan· horxlice wyrmas·
168 sýn scýldigra· ceorfað and slitað·
ne mæg þær æniman· be arnum gewyrhtum·

gedyrstig wesan·¹ deman gehende·

ac ealle þurh yrnð óga æt somne.²
172 breost gehyda· and se bitera wóp·
and þær stænt astifad· stane gelicast·
eal arleas heap· yfelef on wenan ;
hwæt dest þu la flæsc· hwæt dreogeft þu nú·
176 hwæt miht þu on þa tid þearfe gewepan ;
Wa þe nu þu þeowast·
and her glæd leofast. on galnysse
and þe mid stiðum astyrest· sticelum þær gælsan ;
180 Hwi ne forhtas þu fyrene egsan·
and þe sylfum ondræd· swiðlice witu·
ða deoflum geo drihten geteode·
awyrgedum gastum weana to leane·
184 þa oferswiðað· sefan and spræce·
Manna gehwylces for micelnysse
nænig spræc mæg beon· spellum areccan·
ænegum on eorðan· earmlice witu·
188 fule stowa fyres on grunde·
þe wæs in grimmum susle on helle ;
þær fynt to sorge æt somne gemenged·
se þrosma lig· and se þrece gicela
192 swiðe hat and ceald· helle to middes·
hwilum þær éagan ungemetum wepað·
for þæs ofnes bryne· eal he is bealuwes full ;
hwilum eac þa teþ for miclum cyle manna þær
gryrrað ;

There will be the needy, and kings of people,
Poor and rich all will be affrighted.
There will have one law, poor and the wealthy.

Rich and poor
will be judged
alike.

164 Therefore they will have fear all alike.
That angry flood will rush with fire,
And bitterly burn the poor souls:
And the hearts, savagely worms,
168 Of sin-guilty ones, will carve and tear.
Nor may there any man, by works of merit,
Bold become in presence of the Judge;
But terror will run alike through all,

All will be
terrified.

172 Thoughts of the heart, and the bitter weeping.
And there will stand, stiffened most like to stone,
All the wicked troop, in expectation of evil.
What doest thou, O flesh? what actest thou now?

Flesh, thou

176 How might thou on that tide bewail thy trouble?
Woe! thou servest now thyself,
And here gladly livest in lust,

livest now in
lust.

And thyself with keen goads there urgest to luxury.

Wilt thou not
fear hell,

180 Why wilt thou not fear the fiery terror,
And for thyself dread greatly the punishments
Which for devils of yore the Lord prepared
To cursed souls for wages of woe?
184 These overpass thought and speech,
Of every man for greatness.
No speech may be with tidings to recount
To any on earth the wretched penalties,

fire and sulphur,

188 Filthy places of fire in the depth,
That was mid fierce torment in hell.
There be for sorrow together mingled
The flame of vapours, and the weariness of cold,

vapour and cold!

192 Very heat and cold, in midst of hell.
One while there the eyes without measure will weep;
For the scorching of the furnace, he is all full of misery;
One while too the teeth of men for great cold there
    will gnash.

196 þis atule gewrixl· earmsceape men·
    on worulda woruld· wendaᵹ þær inne·
    betwyx forsworcenum sweartum nihtum·

  and weallendes pices· wean & þrosmes¹

200 þær nan stefne styreᵹ butan stearc-heard
    wop· and wanung na-wiht elles·
    ne biᵹ þær ánsyn gesewen. ænigre wihte·
    butan þara cwelra becwylmaᵹ ᵹa earman·

204 ne biᵹ þær ínne áht geméted·
    butan líg· and cyle· and laᵹlic fúl
    hy mid nósan ne magon naht geswæccan·

² MS.unftence.   butan unftences² ormætneffe·

208 þær beoᵹ þa wanigendran· welras gefylde·
    ligspiwelum bryne· laᵹlices fyres
    and hy wæl-grimme· wyrmas slitaᵹ
    and heora ban gnagaᵹ. brynigum tuxlum.

212 Ufenon eal þis biᵹ ꝥ earme breost·
    mid bitere care breged and swenced.
    for hwi fyrgende flæsc· on þas freonan tid
    hym selfum swa fela synna· geworhte·

216 ꝥ hit on cweartern cwylmed wyrde·
    þær ᵹa atelan synd· ecan witu·
    þær leohtef ne leoht lytel sperca·
    earmum ænig· ne þær arfæstnes·

220 ne sib· ne hópa· ne swige· gegladaᵹ·
    ne þara wera worn wihte·
    Flyhᵹ frofor aweg ne biᵹ þær fultum nan·
    ꝥ wiᵹ þa biteran þing· gebeorh mæge fremman ;

224 Ne biᵹ þær ansyn gemet· ænigre blisse·
    ꝥ biᵹ angryslic· ege & fyrhtu·

³ MS.grisgbig-tung.   and sarimod swiᵹlic· gristbitung³
    þær biᵹ unrotnes æghwær wæl-hreow

228 eald· and yrre· and æmelnes
    and þær synne eac. sauwle on lige·
    on blindum fcræfe· byrnaᵹ & yrnaᵹ ;

196 This foul vicissitude, miserable men,
    For ever and ever, will wend therein :
    Amid dark black night
    And the woe of boiling pitch and vapour.
200 There no sound stirreth, save stark hard
    Weeping and lamenting, naught else.
    Nor will be any appearance seen of any wight,
    But of the torturers (which) punish the miserable.

Naught is heard but weeping and woe,

204 Nor will there be therein aught found
    But fire, and cold, and loathsome filth.
 ·   They with nose may naught smell
    Save immensity of stench.

naught smelt but stench.

208 There will be the wretched lips filled
    With flame-vomiting blaze of loathly' fire,
    And the cruel worms will tear them,
    And will gnaw their bones with burning tusks.
212 Above all this will be that wretched breast
    With bitter care frightened and troubled.
    For why luxurious flesh in the perilous tide
    For himself so many sins wrought,
216 That it in prison became destroyed ;
    There are the dreadful everlasting punishments,
    There not any little spark of light shineth
    To the miserable.   There neither goodness
220 Nor peace, nor hope, nor quiet delighteth,
    Nor the number of the men at all.

There is neither peace nor hope,

    Consolation will fly away, nor will there be any help
    That against the bitter circumstances may frame a protection :
224 Nor will there appearance be found of any bliss :
    There will be horrid fear and terror,
    And violent sorrowful gnashing of teeth.
    There will be everywhere cruel sadness,

but terror,

sadness,

228 Eld and anger and weariness,
    And there too sin. Souls in fire
    In the dark cave will burn and wander.

and sin.

þonne deriende gedwinað heonone·
232 þyſſe worulde geféan. gewítað mid ealle·
þonne druncennes· gedwineð mid wiſtum·
and hleahter· and plega· hleapað æt somne·
and wrænnes eac· gewiteð heonone·
236 and fæſthafolnes· feor gewiteð·
uncyſt on-weg· & ælc gælsa·

¹ MS.scyndam.   ſcyldig ſcyndan· [1] on ſceade þone·
& ſe earma flyhð· uncræftiga ſlæp·
240 fléac mid sluman· ſlincan on hinder ;
Ðonne blindum beseah· biterum ligum·
earme on ende. ꝥ unalyfed iſ nu·
² MS. leofes.   leofest [2] on life· lað bið þænne·
.244 and ꝥ werige mod wendað þa gyltaſ.
ſwiðe mid sorgum· and mid sargunge·
Eala ſe bið gesælig and ofer sælig.
³ MS. wihtna.   & on worulda woruld· wihta [3] gesæligoſt·
248 ſe þe mid gesyntum· ſwylce cwyldas·
and witum mæg· wel forbugon·
and samod bliðe· on woruld ealle·
hiſ þeodne geþeon· & þonne mot habban
252 heofonrice· ꝥ is hihta mæst·
þær niht ne genipð· næfre þeostra·
þæs heofenlican leohtes sciman·
ne cymð þær sorh ne sár· ne geſwenced yld·
256 ne þær ænig geſwinc· æfre gelimpeð·
oððe hunger· oððe þurst· oððe heanlic slæp·
ne bið þær fefur· ne adl· ne færlic cwyld·
naneſ liges gebrasl· ne ſe laðlica cyle·
260 nis þær unrotnes· ne þær æmelnys·
ne hryre· ne caru· ne hreoh tintrega·
ne bið þær liget. ne laðlic storm·
winter· ne þunerrad· ne wiht cealdes·
⁴ MS. swa se. 264 ne þær hagul ſcuras hearde mid snawe [4]
ne bið þær wædl· ne lyre· ne deaðes gryre·

Then will perish from hence the fatal
232 Joys of this world; they will depart all together.
Then drunkenness will cease with feasts,
And laughter and play will leap together.
And lust also will depart hence,
236 And greed will far depart,
Wickedness away, and each luxury,
Guilty to hasten into the shade.
And the wretched helpless sleep will fly,
240 Slack with slumber, to slink behind.
Then in dark bitter fire saw
The poor at last, that which forbidden is now;
That most loved in life, loathed will be then,
244 And the guilts will turn that weary heart
Verily among sorrows and among misery.
Oh! he will be happy, and more than happy,
And world-without-end of men the happiest,
248 He that with prosperity, such overthrow,
And with understanding, may well escape,
And likewise blessed in all the world
Serve his lord, and then may have
252 Heaven's kingdom, that is of joys the best.
There night nor darkness overclouds
The sheen of heavenly light.
There cometh not sorrow nor pain, nor toilworn eld,
256 Nor happeth there ever any toil;
Either hunger, or thirst, or miserable sleep.
There is not fever, nor decay, nor sudden plague,
Crackling of no fire, nor the loathsome cold,
260 There is not mourning, nor there weariness,
Nor ruin, nor care, nor fierce torment.
Nor is there lightning, nor loathsome storm,
Winter, nor thunder shower, nor a whit of cold;
264 Nor there are mighty hail-showers with snow,
Nor is want there, nor loss, nor terror of death,

*Marginal glosses:*
Worldly joys there vanish,
and the desire of life be loathed.
Happy will be he who with
wit escapes this hell,
and gains God's heaven,
where comes not sorrow or pain,
mourning or care,
want, or death.

2

ne yrmð· ne agnes· ne nænigu gnornung

Ac þær samod ricxað· sib mid spede·

268 and arfæstnes· and ece god·

wuldor· and wurðmynt·

swylce lof· and lif· and leoflic geþwærnes·[1]

Ufenan eal þis éce drihten him ealra

272 goda gehwylc· glædlice ðenað ;

þæra andweard ealle wcorðaþ and fehþ·

and geblyfað fæder ætsomne· wuldraþ and wel hylt·

fægere frætuað· and freolice lufað·

276 & in heofon-fetle· heah gehrineð·[2]

his sunu bliðe· sigores brytta·

fylð anragehwam· ece mede·

heofonlice hyrfta· ꝥ is healic gifu·

280 gemang þam ænlican engla werode·

and þæra haligra heapum and þreatum[3]

þær hy beoð geþeode þeodfcipum on gemang·

betwyx heahfæderas· and halige witegan·

284 blissiendum modum· byrgum to middes·

þær þa ærendracan synd· ælmihtiges godes·

and betweoh rofena reade heapaf·

þær symle scinað·

288 þær þæra hwittra hwyrfð mæden-heap·

bloftmum behangen· beortost wereda

þe ealle læt ænlicu godes drut·

feo frowe þe us frean acende·

292 metod on moldan· meowle seo clæne·

þæt is MARÍA· mædena felast·

heo let þurh þa scenan scinendan rícu·

gebletsodost ealra. þæs breman fæder·

296 betweox fæder and sunu· freolicum werede·

and betwyx þære écan uplicum sibbe·

rice rædwitan rodera-weardes ;[4]

hwæt mæg beon heardes her on life·

---

[1] gehþwærnes MS.

[2] MS. heah gerinnað.

[3] þreapum MS.

[4] MS. weardas.

Nor misery, nor sorrow, nor any mourning.

But there together reigneth peace with prosperity, But ever peace

268 And virtue, and eternal good,

Glory and honour,

Likewise praise, and life, and faithful concord.

Beside all this the Eternal Lord to them of all

272 Goods any gladly serveth,

And in presence honoureth and receiveth all of them ;

And the Father likewise blesseth, glorifieth, and well- the blessing of God,

regardeth (them),

Beautifully decks, and liberally loveth,

276 And on heaven's throne on high adorneth.

His kind Son, lord of Victory, the gift of Christ,

Gives to each one everlasting meed,

Heavenly glories, that is a splendid gift.

280 Among the beautiful host of angels, the fellowship of angels,

And in troops and throngs of the holy ones,

There shall they be associated among nations,

Amidst the patriarchs and holy prophets.

284 In blissful mood among the cities,

There be the apostles of Almighty God.

And amid the stores of roses red

There ever shall they shine.

288 There of the white ones shall wander a maiden throng the company of virgins,

With blossoms hung. Brightest of the hosts,

Who them all will lead, God's peerless dear one, led by

The woman who for us the Lord conceived,

292 Creator on earth : virgin the pure,

That is MARY, of maidens most blessed. Mary, mother of God.

She will lead through those bright shining kingdoms

(Blessedest she of all) of the glorious father,

296 Betwixt father and son, a goodly host,

And mid eternal heavenly peace,

In the kingdom of the wise heavenly ruler. What are earth's hardships to this ?

What of hardship can there be here in life,

300 Gif þu wille secgan soð þæm ðe frineð·
     wið þam þu mote· gemang þam werode·
     eardian unbleoh· on ecnesse·
     and on upcundra· eadegum setlum·
304 brucan bliðnesse butan ende forð·

*Her endað þeof boc þe hatte inter florigeras ðæt is on englisc
betwyx blowende þe to godes rice farað. and hu ða þrowiað
þe to helle farað.*

300 If thou wilt say sooth to him that asketh thee
    To set against this, that thou mayest, among that host,
    Live unchanging through eternity,
    And in the happy seats of the saints above
304 Enjoy bliss henceforth without end.

Thou mayst live in bliss without an end.

Here endeth this book that is called inter florigeras, *that is, in English, "betwixt blooming," who to God's Kingdom fare: and how those suffer, who to Hell fare.*

DE DIE JUDICII.

[From Migne's Edition of BEDE, Vol. V. p. 634.]

Inter florigeras fecundi cespitis herbas,
Flamine ventorum resonantibus undique ramis,
Arboris umbriferæ mæstus sub tegmine solus
4 Dum sedi, subito planctu turbatus amaro,
Carmina præ tristi cecini hæc lugubria mente
Utpote commemorans scelerum commissa meorum,
Et maculas vitæ, mortisque inamabile tempus,
8 Judiciique diem horrendo examine magnum,
Perpetuamque reis districti judicis iram,
Et genus humanum discretis sedibus omne,
Gaudia sanctorum necnon, pœnasque malorum.
12 Hæc memorans mecum tacito sub murmure dixi:
Nunc rogo, nunc venæ fontes aperite calentes,
Dumque ego percutiam pugnis rea pectora, vel dum
Membra solo sternam, meritosque ciebo dolores,
16 Vos, precor, effusis lacrymis non parcite statim,
Sed mœstam salsis faciem perfundite guttis.
Et reserate nefas Christo cum voce gementi,
Nec lateat quidquam culparum cordis in antro.
20 Omnia quin luci verbis reddantur apertis,
Pectoris et linguæ, carnis vel crimina sæva.
Hæc est sola salus animæ, et spes certa dolenti,
Vulnera cum lacrymis medico reserare superno;

24 Qui solet allisos sanàre et solvere vinctos,
   Quassatos nec vult calamos infringere dextra
   Nec lini tepidos undis exstinguere fumos.
   Nonne exempla tibi pendens dabat in cruce latro
28 Peccati quantum valeat confessio vera ?
   Qui fuit usque crucem sceleratis impius actis,
   Mortis in articulo sed verba precantia clamat,
   Et solo meruit fidei sermone salutem,
32 Cum Christo et portas paradisi intravit apertas.
   Cur rogo, mens, tardas medico te pandere totam ?
   Vel cur lingua, taces, veniæ dum tempus habebis ?
   Auribus Omnipotens te nunc exaudit apertis.
36 Ille dies veniet, judex dum venerit orbis
   Debebis qua tu rationem reddere de te.
   Suadeo prævenias lacrymis modo judicis iram.
   Quid tu in sorde jaces, scelerum caro plena piaclis ?
40 Cur tua non purgas lacrymis peccata profusis
   Et tibi non oras placidæ fomenta medelæ ?
   Fletibus assiduis est dum data gratia flendi,
   Pœnituisse juvat tibi nunc et flere salubre est.
44 Æternus fuerit placidus te vindice judex.
   Nec Deus ætherius bis crimina vindicat ulli,
   Spernere tu noli veniæ tibi tempora certa.
   Quanta malis maneant etiam tormenta memento,
48 Vel quam celsithronus metuendus ab arce polorum
   Adveniet judex, mercedem reddere cunctis,
   Præcurrent illum vel qualia signa, repente
   Terra tremet, montesque ruent, collesque liquescent
52 Et mare terribili confundet murmure mentes.
   Tristius et cœlum tenebris obducitur atris,
   Astra cadunt rutilo et Titan tenebrescit in ortu.
   Pallida nocturnam nec præstat luna lucernam,
56 De cœlo venient et signa minantia mortem,
   Tum superum subito veniet commota potestas,
   Cœtibus angelicis regem stipata supernum.

Ille sedens solio fulget sublimis in alto,
60 Ante illum rapimur, collectis undique turmis,
Judicium ut capiat gestorum quisque suorum.
Sis memor illius, qui tum pavor ante tribunal
Percutiet stupidis cunctorum corda querelis.
64 Dum simul innumeris regem comitata polorum
Angelica advenient coelestibus agmina turmis,
Atque omnes pariter homines cogentur adesse,
Qui sunt, qui fuerant, fuerint vel quique futuri
68 Cunctaque cunctorum cunctis arcana patebunt.
Quod cor, lingua, manus tenebrosis gessit in antris
Et quod nunc aliquem verecundans scire veretur
Omnibus in patulo pariter tunc scire licebit.
72 Insuper impletur flammis altricibus aer,
Ignis ubique suis ruptis regnabit habenis.
Et quo nunc aer gremium diffundit inane
Ignea tunc sonitus perfundet flamma feroces,
76 Festinans scelerum saevas ulciscere causas.
Nec vindex ardor cuiquam tunc parcere curat,
Sordibus ablutus veniat nisi ab omnibus illuc.
Tunc tribus et populi ferient rea pectora pugnis
80 Stabit uterque simul stupidus, pauperque potensque
Et miser et dives simili ditione timebunt:
Fluvius ignivomus miseros torquebit amare
Et vermes scelerum mordebunt intima cordis.
84 Nullus ibi meritis confidit judice praesens,
Singula sed nimius percurrit pectora terror
Et stupet attonito simul impia turba timore.
Quid, caro, quid facies, illâ quid flebilis horâ
88 Quæ modo væ misera servire libidine gaudes,
Luxuriæque tuæ stimulis te agitabis acutis
Ignea tu tibimet cur non tormenta timebis,
Dæmonibus dudum fuerantque parata malignis.
92 Quæ superant sensus cunctorum et dicta virorum,
Nec vox ulla valet miseras edicere poenas,

Ignibus æternæ nigris loca plena gehennæ,
Frigora mista simul ferventibus algida flammis
96 Nunc oculos nimio flentes ardore camini
Nunc iterum nimio stridentes frigore dentes.
Iis miseris vicibus miseri volvuntur in ævum
Obscuras inter picea caligine noctes.
100 Vox ubi nulla sonat, durus nisi fletus ubique,
Non nisi tortorum facies ubi cernitur ulla.
Non sentitur ibi quidquam nisi frigora, flammæ
Fœtor et ingenti complet putredine nares.
104 Os quoque flammivomum lugens implebitur igne,
Et vermes lacerant ignitis dentibus ossa.
Insuper et pectus curis torquetur amaris,
Cur caro luxurians sibimet sub tempore parvo
108 Atro perpetuas meruisset carcere pœnas;
Lucis ubi miseris nulla scintilla relucet
Nec pax nec pietas immo spes nulla quietis
Flentibus arrident, fugiunt solatia cuncta.
112 Auxilium nullus rebus præstabit amaris,
Lætitiæ facies jam nulla videbitur illic
Sed dolor et gemitus, stridor, pavor, et timor horrens,
Tædia, tristitiæ, trux indignatio, languor.
116 Errantesque animæ flammis in carcere cæco.
Noxia tunc hujus cessabunt gaudia sæcli,
Ebrietas, epulæ, risus, petulantia, jocus,
Dira cupido, tenax luxus, scelerata libido,
120 Somnus iners torporque gravis, desidia pigra
Illicitat quidquid modo delectatio carnis
Et cæca scelerum mergit vertigine mentem,
Tunc cæcis merget flammis sine fine misellos.
124 Felix o nimium, semperque in sæcula felix
Qui illas effugiet pœnarum prospere clades
Cum sanctisque simul lætatur in omnia sæcla !
Conjunctus Christo cœlestia regna tenebit,
128 Nox ubi nulla rapit splendorem lucis amœnæ,

Non dolor aut gemitus veniet, nec fessa senectus
Non sitis, esuries, somnus et non labor ullus
Non febris, morbi, clades, non frigora, flammæ
132 Tædia, tristitiæ, curæ, tormenta, ruinæ
Fulmina, nimbus, hiems, tonitru, nix, grando, procella,
Angor, paupertas, mœror, mors, casus, egestas,
Sex pax et pietas, bonitas, opulentia regnat,
136 Gaudia, lætitiæ, virtus, lux, vita perennis
Gloria, laus, requies, honor et concordia dulcis,
Insuper omne bonum cunctis Deus ipse ministrat.
Semper adest præsens, cunctos fovet, implet, honorat,
140 Glorificat, servat, veneratur, diligit, ornat,
Collocat Altithrono, lætosque in sede polorum
Præmia perpetuis tradens cœlestia donis.
Angelicas inter turmas sanctasque cohortes
144 Vatidicis junctos patriarchis atque prophetis
Inter apostolicas animis lœtantibus arces.
Atque inter roseis splendentia castra triumphis
Candida virgineo simul inter agmina flore.
148 Quæ trahit alma Dei genetrix, pia Virgo Maria,
Per benedicta Patris fulgenti regua paratu
Inter et Ecclesiæ sanctos, natosque, patresque,
Inter et ætherium cœlesti pace senatum.
152 Quid, rogo, quid durum, sæclo consetur in isto,
Utque illas inter liceat habitare cohortes,
Sedibus et superum semper gaudere beatis ?
Incolumem mihi te Christi charissima proles,
156 Protegat, et faciat semper sine fine beatam
Meque tuis Christo precibus commenda benignis.

Lár.

(AN EXHORTATION.)

LÁR.

[Immediately after the previous version, the MS. has the following lines.]

Nu lære ic þe fwa man leofne fceal·
gif þu wille that blowende ríce gestigan·
þænne beo þu eadmod· & ælmes georn·
4 wis on wordum· and wæccan lufa·
on hyge halgum. on þas hwilwendan tid·
bliðe mode· and gebedum filige·
oftost symle· þær þu ana sy·
8 forðan ꝥ halige gebed· and seo hluttre lufu·
godes and manna. and seo ælmes sylen· and se miccla
hopa
to þinum hælende· ꝥ he þine fynna
adwæfcan wylle· and eac oþera fela
12 godra weorca· glengað and bringað.
þa soðfæstan sauwle to reste.
on þa uplican eadignesse·
Wyrc ꝥ þu wyrce· word oððe dæda·
16 hafa metodes ege· on gemang fymle·
ꝥ is witodlice wisdomes ord·
ꝥ þu ꝥ ece leoht· eal ne forleose·
þeos woruld is æt ende· and we synd wædlan gýt·
20 heofena rices· ꝥ is hefig byrdæn.
and þeah þu æfter þinum ende eall gesylle·
ꝥ þu on eorðan ær gestryndes·
goda gehwylces· wylle gode cweman·
24 ne mihtu mid þæm eallum· saule þine

EXHORTATION.

Now I teach thee as one shall do a beloved one.

If thou wilt attain that blooming realm,

Then be thou humble, and bountiful, *If thou wilt
heaven win,*

4 Wise in words, and love watchfulness.

In holy thought, in the present time, *be holy, kind,
and pray.*

Kind of disposition, and abundant in prayers,

Continually when thou art alone.

8 Because holy prayer, and pure love

Of God and man, and almsgiving, and the great
   trust

In thy Saviour, that he thy sins

Will erase, and likewise many other

12 Good works adorn and bring

The upright soul to rest

In heavenly happiness.

Work what thou workest, word or deed ; *Work; fear God.*

16 Have fear of the Creator, in the midst,

That is assuredly the beginning of wisdom,

That thou the everlasting light all do not lose.

This world is fleeting, and we are yet poor

20 Of heaven's kingdom. That is a heavy burden.

And though thou after thine end give everything *Trust not to
death-bed
alms.*

That thou on earth before acquiredst

Of each good, will it please God ?

24 Nor might thou, with the whole, thy soul

ut alyfan gif heo inne wyrð
feondum befangen· frofre bedæled·
welena forwynned· ac þu wuldres god·
28 éce ælmihtigne· ealninga bidde·
ꝥ he þe ne forlæte· laðum to handa·
feondum to frofre· ac þu fleoh þanan·
syle ælmesfan. oft and gelome.
32 digolice ꝥ við drihtnes lár·
gumena gehwylcef· þo on god gelyfð;
Ceapa þe mid æhtum eces leohtes·
þy læs þu forweorðe· þænne þu hyra
geweald
36 nafast to syllanne· hit bið swiðe yfel
manna gehwilcum· ꝥ he micel age·
gif he him god ne ondræt·
fwiðor micle· þonne his sylfes gewil·
40 Warna þe georne wið þære wambe fylle·
forþan heo þa unþeawaf ealle gesomnað·
þe þære saule fwiðoft deriað·
ꝥ if druncennef· and dyrne geligere·
44 ungemet wilnung. ætef· & flæpef·
þa man mæg mid fæftenum·
and forhæfdnessum heonon adrifan·
and mid cyric focnum cealdum wederum·
48 eadmodlice· ealluncga biddan·
heófena drihten· ꝥ he þe hæl gife.
milde mund bora· fwa him gemet þince·
and ondræd þu ðe dihle wifan·
52 nearwe geþancaf· þe on niht becumað·
fyn luftaf for-oft· fwiðe fremman·
earfoðlice· þy þu earhlice fcealt·
gyltas þine· fwiðe bemurnan.
56 har hilderinc· hefie þe ðincaþ·
fynna þine· forþam þu sylf ongýte·
ꝥ þu alætan fcealt· læne fcaþelaf·

Release, if it become among
Fiends captured, of comfort bereft,
Of wealth deprived. But do thou the God of glory,

28 The eternal almighty, constantly pray
That he let thee not fall into the hands of evil ones,
To the gain of fiends. But flee thou from thence,
Give alms, oft and repeatedly, in secret,

32 That is the exhortation of the Lord,
For each man that believes in God.
Buy for thyself eternal light with thy possessions,
The less wilt thou be undone, when thou the power
over them

36 Hast not to give. It is very evil
To every man that he have much,
If he fear not God
Much more than his own will.

40 Take thou good heed against gluttony,
For it assembleth all the bad qualities
Which most destroy the soul,
That is, drunkenness and secret fornication,

44 Undue longing for food and sleep.
These man may with fasting
And continence drive away,
And with church going in cold weather.

48 Humbly always [take care] to pray
The Lord of heaven, that he give thee health,
The kind protector, as to him seems fit ;
And be thou afraid of secret plans,

52 Of troublesome thoughts, that arise at night,
Sinful desires oftentimes greatly to produce.
With trouble therefore thou in terror shalt
Thy offences greatly mourn.

56 Grey-haired warrior, heavy seem to thee
Thy sins. Therefore do thou thyself understand
That thou shalt leave thy gifts unharmed,

*Side notes:*

They will not rescue thee from friends.

Pray;

give alms oft in thy life;

buy thyself heaven with thy goods on earth.

Guard against gluttony.

Drive it off with fasting, and church-going in the cold.

Fear too bad thoughts at night.

eard. and eþel· uncuð bið þe þænne·

60 to hwan þe þin drihten gedon wille·

þænne þu lengc ne moſt· lifeſ brucan·

eardes on eþle· swa þu ær dydest·

blissum hremi· nu þu ðe beorgan scealt·

64 and wið feonda gehwæne· fæſtc healdan·

ſauwle þine· á hi winnað embe

¹ dæges & nihtes· ongean drihtnes líf ;

þú miht hy gefleman gif þu filian wilt·

68 larum minum. swa ic lære þe

digollice· ꝥ þu on dægred·

oft ymbe þynre´ſauwle ræd· swiðe ſmeage·

hu þu ꝥ ece leoht. æfre begytan mæge.

72 síðe geſécan· þu ſcealt glædlice· ſwiðe ſwincan·

wið þæs úplican· éþelríceſ·

dægeſ & nihteſ· þu scealt drúncen fleon·

and þa oferfylle· ealle forlætan·

76 gif þu wilt þa úpplican eárdwic ceosan·

þænne ſcealt þu hit on eórðan ǽr geþencan·

and þu þe ſylfne· ſwiðe gebinde·

and þa unþeawaſ· ealle forlætan·

80 þe þu on þiſ life· ær lufedest & feddest·

¹ ꝥ added in MS.

Land and country.   Unknown to thee then will be
60 Whither thy lord will assign thee ;
   When thou no longer mayest enjoy life   *Thou canst not live long.*
   In earth's region, as thou didst before
   Exulting in bliss.   Now oughtest thou to save thyself, *Save thyself then!*
64 And against every enemy hold fast
   Thy soul.   Ever they labour around,
   By day and night, against the lord's life.
   Thou mightest put them to flight, if thou wilt follow *Rout thy soul's foes!*
68 My teaching, as I teach thee—
   Secretly that thou in the early morn
   Oft for thy soul's advantage earnestly meditate
   How thou the eternal light ever mayest attain ;
72 With pains to seek, thou shalt gladly eagerly labour *Seek the kingdom of heaven.*
   After the heavenly kingdom ;
   By day and night, thou shalt drunkenness flee, *Flee drunkenness, gluttony,*
   And gluttony all forego.
76 If thou wilt that heavenly land choose,
   Then shalt thou on earth before think on it,
   And earnestly restrain thyself,
   And forego all bad habits *and all thy old bad habits.*
80 Which thou in life formerly didst love and cherish.

Oratio Poetica.

Thænne gemiltsað þe· N. mundum qui regit·
ðeoda þrym-Cyningc· Thronum sedens[1]
a butan ende·
4 saule wine·
Geunne þe on life· Auctor pacis·
Sibbe gesælða· salus mundi·
metod se inæra· magna virtute·
8 & se soðfæsta· summi filius·
fo on fultum· factor cosmi·
se of æðelre wæs· virginis partu·
Clæne acenned· Christus in orbem·
12 Metod þurh MARIAN· Mundi redemptor·
& þurh þæne halgan gast· voca frequenter·
Bide helpes hine· Clementem Dominum·[2]
Sé onsénded wæs· Summo de throno·
16 & þære clænan· Clara voce·
þe gebyrd-boda· bona voluntate·
ꝥ heo scolde cennan· Christum regem·
Ealra cyninga cyningc· Casta vivendo·
20 & þu þa soð-fæstan· Supplex roga·[3]
fultumes bidde fricolo· Virginem almam·
& þær æfter tó· omnes sanctos[4]
Blið-mod bidde· Beatos et justos·[5]
24 ꝥ hi ealle þe· Unica voce
þingian to þeodne· Thronum regentem
Ecum drihtne· Alta polorum
ꝥ he þine saule· Summus judex
28 On-fo freolice· factor æternus·
& he gelæde· in lucem perennem[6]
þær eadige· Animæ sanctæ·
Rice restað· Regnis[7] cælorum·

[1] MS. sedentem.

[2] MS. Dominus.

[3] MS. rogo.

[4] MS. sanctus.

[5] MS. justus.

[6] MS. luce.

ORATIO POETICA.

Then He who rules the world shall have mercy upon thee (N),
He, the glorious King of the nations, who sitteth upon the throne,
Ever without end,   Invocation of
the Father.
4 The friend of the soul.
May He—the Author of peace—grant thee, in thy life,
The joys of peace—(He who is) the Health of the world,
The famous Lord, of great power !
8 And may the faithful Son of the Highest,
Maker of the universe, receive (thee) into favour,
Who was, by birth from the noble Virgin,   Invocation of
the Son.
Purely brought forth, as Christ, into the world.
12 Lord and Redeemer of the world—by means of Mary,
And through the Holy Ghost !
Call upon Him [the Holy Ghost] often,   Invocation of
the Holy Ghost.
Pray to Him for help (who is a) merciful Lord,
16 Who was sent-down from the highest throne,
And (was) to the pure one [Mary] (by His) clear voice
The messenger of (Christ's) birth, with good will,
That she should bring forth Christ the King,
20 (She) chaste of life (bring forth) the King of all kings,
And thou, suppliantly beseech the true one,
Pray for help fervently to the benign Virgin.   Invocation of
the Virgin.
And thereafter moreover all the saints,   Invocation of
All Saints.
24 Blithe of mood, invoke, the blessed and just ones,
That they for thee all, with one accord,
May intercede to the Lord who rules upon the throne,
(To the) eternal Lord, (who rules) the high places of the skies,
28 That He, the Supreme Judge, thy soul   Final result.
Will freely receive, (He who is) the Eternal Creator,
And may He lead (thee) to perennial light,
Where the blessed sainted souls
32 Rest in the kingdom, the kingdom of heaven !

Paraphrasis Poetica in Orationem Dominicam.

PARAPHRASIS POETICA IN ORATIONEM DOMINICAM.

Pater noster.

Þu éart ure fæder ealles wealdend·
Cyninc on wuldre· forðam we clypiað to þe·
áre biddað nu ðu ýþost miht·
4 sawle alysan þu híg sændest áer·
þurh þine æþelan hand into þam flæsce
ac hwar cymð heo nú·
buton þu engla god eft hiӡ alýse·
8 sawle of synnum þurh ðine soðan miht.

Qui es in celis.

Ðu eart on heofonum· hiht and frofor·
Blissa beorhtost· ealle [1] abúgað to þe
þinra gasta þrym· anre stæfne·
12 clypiað to criste cweþað ealle þus
halig eart þu halig· heofon-engla cyningc·
drihten úre· & þine domas synd
rihte & rume· ræcað [2] efne gehwam
16 æӡhwilcum men agen gewyrhta·
wel bið ðam þe wyrcð willan þinne.

Sanctificetur nomen tuum.

Swa is gehalgod þin heah nama·
swiðe mærlice manegum gereordum· [3]
20 twa & hund seofontig· þæs þe secgað bec·
ꝥ þu engla god· ealle gesettest·
ælcere þeode· þeaw & wisan·
þa wurþiað þin weorc· wordum and dædum·
24 þurh gecynd clypiað· & crist heriað·
& þin lof lædað lifigenda god·
swa þu eart geæþelod· geond ealle world.

POETICAL PARAPHRASE OF THE LORD'S PRAYER.

Pater noster.

Thou art our father, Ruler of all,   Our Father,
King in Glory, therefore we cry to thee :
For mercy we pray, now thou canst most easily
4 Release our soul, thou before dost send it
Through thy noble hand into the flesh.
But where will it come now,
Unless thou God of Angels again release it :
8 The soul from sins through thy trusty might ?

Qui es in celis.

Thou art in heaven, hope and consolation,   Which art in
Brightest of joys, to thee bow down,   heaven,
The host of all thy spirits.   With one voice
12 They cry to Christ ; they all thus exclaim,
Holy art Thou, holy, King of heaven's angels,
Our Lord ; and Thy judgments are
Right and ample.   They extend yea to each,
16 Each single man, [judgments] for his own works.
Blessed will he be that worketh thy will.

Sanctificetur nomen tuum.

Thy lofty name is so hallowed,   Hallowed be
Very famously in many tongues   thy name.
20 Two and seventy, as the books tell
That thou God of angels all arrangedst
Of each people, the manners and customs ;
These praise thy work in words and deeds,
24 Through nature they call on and praise Christ
And thy praise they set forth, oh living God,
So thou art honoured through all the world.

Adveniat regnum tuum.

Cum nu & mildsa· mihta waldend·
28 & us þin rice alyf· rihtwis dema
Earda selost & ece lif
þar we sib and lufe[1] samod gemetað·
eagena beorhtnys· & ealle mirhðe·
32 þer bið gehyred þin halige lof·
& þin micele miht mannum to frofre·
swa þu engla god eallum blissast·

Fiat voluntas tua.

Gewurðe þin willa· swa þu waldend eart·
36 éce geopenod· geond ealle world·
& þu þe silf eart sodfæst dema·
rice rædbora· geond rumne grund·
swa þin heahsetl is· heah and mære·
40 fæger & wurðlic· swa þin fæder worhte·
æþele & éce· þar ðu on sittest
on þinre swiðran healf· þu eart sunu & fæder
ana ægþer· swa is þin æþele[2] gecynd·
44 Micclum gemærsod· & þu monegum helpst·
ealra cyninga þrym· clypast ofer ealle·
bið þin wuldor-word· wide gehyred·
þonne þu þine fyrde fægere geblissast·
48 sylest miht and mund· micclum herige·
and þe þánciað ðusenda fela·
eal engla þrym anre stæfne.

Sicut in celo.

Swa þe on heofonum· heah þrymnesse·
52 æþele & éce á þanciað·
clæne & gecorene· cristes þegnas·
singað & biddað· soðfæstne god·
are & gifnesse· ealre þeode·
56 þonne þu him tiðast týreadig cyninge·

Adveniat regnum tuum.

Come now and pity, Ruler of might,
Thy kingdom come.
28 And grant us thy kingdom, righteous judge,
Happiest of homes, and eternal life.
There we shall find peace and love together,
Brightness of eyes and all mirth :
32 There will be heard thy holy praise,
And thy great might, for consolation to men,
So thou, God of Angels, blessest all.

Fiat voluntas tua.

Let thy will done, as thou art Sovereign,
Thy will be done
36 Eternally revealed, over all the world,
And thou thyself art righteous judge,
Mighty counsellor, over the wide earth :
So is thy high throne, high and grand
40 Fair and honourable : as thy father wrought
Noble and eternal, where Thou sittest
On thy own right hand. Thou art Son and Father,
Both persons in one ; so is thy noble nature
44 Much magnified ; and thou helpest many,
Thou, the might of all kings, thou callest above all,
Thy word of might is heard afar.
When thou thy host joyously makest happy,
48 Thou givest might and protection to the great army,
And many thousands thank thee,
The host of all angels with one voice.

Sicut in celo.

As in heaven in majesty
As in heaven,
52 The noble and immortal servants of Christ
Pure and elect ever thank thee :
They sing and pray to the righteous God
For mercy and the forgiveness of all people ;
56 Then thou grantest to them, glorious king,

swa þu eadmod eart ealre worlde·
sy þe þanc & lof· þinre mildse
wuldor & willa· þu gewurþod eart·
60 on heófonrice heah casere.

Et in terra.

And on eorðan ealra cyninga·
help & heafod· halig léce·
rúðe & riht wis· rum heort hláford·
64 þu geæþelodest þe ealle gesceafta·
& tosyndrodest hig· siððan on manega·
sealdest ælcre gecynd agene wisan
& a þine mildse ofer manna bearn

Panem nostrum cotidianum.

68 Swa mid sibbe sænst urne hlaf
dæghwamlice duguðe þinre·
rihtlice dælest
mete þinum mannum· & him mare gehætst·
72 æfter forðsiðe· þines fæder rice·
ꝥ wæs on fruman· fægere gegearwod·
earda selost & éce lif·
gif we soð & riht symle gelæstað·

Da nobis hodie.

76 Syle us to dæg· drihten þine
mildse· and mihta· and ure mod gebig·
þanc & þeawas on þín gewil·
bewyrc us on heortan· haligne gast
80 fæste on innan· & us fultum sile·
ꝥ we moton wyrcan willan þinne·
& þe betæcan tyr-eadig cyninge·
sawle ure on þines silfes hand·

Et dimitte nobis debita nostra.

84 Forgif ús ure synna ꝥ ús ne scamige eft·
drihten úre þonne þu on dóme sitst·

As thou art merciful to all the world.
Let there be to thee thanks and praise for thy goodness,
Thou glory and joy! Thou art praised,
60 In the kingdom of heaven as mighty sovereign.

Et in terra.

And on earth of all kings   So in earth.
The help and head, holy healer,
Stedfast and righteous, large-hearted lord.
64 Thou madest for thyself all creatures very good,
And scatteredst them afterwards abroad,
 · Thou gavest each race its peculiar habits,
And ever thy mercy [thou gavest] over the children of men.

Panem nostrum cotidianum.

68 So with peace thou sendest our loaf   Our daily bread
To thy people daily,
Thou rightly apportionest
Meat to thy men, and to them promisest more
72 After their departure; the kingdom of thy father,
That was in the beginning fairly prepared,
Happiest of homes, and everlasting life,
If we truth and right always perform.

Da nobis hodie.

76 Grant us to-day, Lord,   Give us to-day.
Thy mercy and power, and incline our heart,
Thought and disposition to thy will.
Establish firmly for us in our heart the Holy Ghost within.
80 And grant us help that we may work thy will.
And that we entrust to thee, glorious king,
Our souls into thine own hand.

Et dimitte nobis debita nostra.

84 Forgive us our sins, that we be not hereafter ashamed, And forgive us
Our Lord, when thou in judgment sittest,   our trespasses,

& ealle men up arisað·
þe fram wife· & fram were· wurdan acænned·
88 beoð þa gebrosnodon eft· bán mid þam flæsce·
ealle ansunde eft geworden·
þar we swutollice sið ðan on cnawað
eal ꝥ we geworhton on worldrice·   ◆

¹ MS. búta.   92 betere· & wyrse· ðar beoð bútu¹ ꝣeara·
ne magon we hit na dýrnan forðam þe hit drihten wat·
and þar gewitnesse beoð wuldor micele·
heofon waru· & eorð waru· hel waru þridde
96 þonne beoð egsa· geond ealle world·
þar man us tyhhað on dæg twegen eardas·
drihtenes áre oð ðe deofles þeowet
swa hwaðer wé geearniað her on life·
100 þa hwile þe ure mihta mæste wæron.

Sicut & nos dimittimus debitoribus nostris.

Ac ðonne us alyseð lifigende god·
sawle ure· swa we her gifað
² MS. agilt.   earmon mannum· þe wið us agiltað·²

Et ne nos inducas in temtationem.

104 And na us þu ne læt· laðe beswícan·
on costunga· cwellan & bearnan·
Sawle ure· þeah we sinna fela·
didon for ure disige· dæges & nihtes
108 idele spræce· & unriht weorc·
þine bodu bræcon· wé þe biddað nu
ælmihtig god· áre & gifnes·
ne læt swa héanlice þin hand geweorc
112 on énde dæge eal forwurðan·

Sed libera nos a malo.

Ac alys us of yfele· ealle we beþurfon
godes gifnesse· agylt habbað·

And all men rise up
That from woman and from man have been born ;
88 Again the wasted bones with the flesh
Shall become whole again.
There we shall clearly know hereafter
All that we wrought in this world,
92 Better and worse, both at hand;
And we may not conceal it, because the Lord knows it,
And there as witnesses will be wondrous many
People of heaven, people of earth, and thirdly people of hell.
96 Then will be terror through all the world,
Then some one will assign to us at that day two conditions,
Either the favour of the Lord, or the service of the devil,
According as we shall have earned either here in life
100 While our powers were at the best.

Sicut et nos dimittimus debitoribus nostris.

And then the living God will deliver for us   *As we forgive
Our souls, as we here forgive   them that tres-
To frail men who offend against us.   pass against us.*

Et ne nos inducas in temtationem.

104 And let not evil beguile us   *And lead us not
In temptation, [and] destroy and burn   into temptation.*
Our souls : though we many sins
Did through our folly day and night,
108 Idle speech, and wrongful work.
We brake thy commands.   We pray thee now,
Almighty God, for mercy and forgiveness ;
Let not so miserably thine handy work
112 At the last day all perish.

Sed libera nos a malo.

But deliver us from evil.   We all need   *But deliver us
God's forgiveness, we have offended   from evil.*

    & swiðe gesingod· we ðe soðfæstan god

116 hæriað· and lofuð· swa þu hælend eart

    cynebearn gecydd· cwycum & deadum·

    æþele & éce ofer ealle þingc·

    þu miht on ánre hand· eaðe befealdan·

120 ealne middan eard swilc is mære cyningc·

Amen.

Sy swa þu silf wilt· soðfæst dema·

wé þe engla god ealle heriað

Swa þu eart gewurðod a on worlda forð.

And sinned much, we thee, the faithful God,
116 Laud and praise.   As thou the Saviour art,
Revealed to quick and dead, as a Royal son,
Noble and eternal, above all things,
Thou in one hand canst easily enfold
120 All the world.   Such is the glorious King.

Amen.

Be it as thou thyself wilt, faithful judge.   Amen.
We all laud thee, God of angels,
As thou art honoured, world without end.

Paraphrasis Poetica in Doxologiam.

PARAPHRASIS POETICA IN DOXOLOGIAM.

Gloria.

Sy þe wuldor & lof· wide geopnod
geond ealle þeoda· þanc & willa
mægen and mildse· & ealles modes lufu·
4 soþfæstra sib· and þines silfes dóm·
world gewlitegod· swa þu wealdan miht
eall eorðan mægen· & uplifte
wind· & wolcna wealdest ealle on riht·

Patri et filio et Spiritui Sancto.

8 Ðu éart frofra fæder· & feorhhyrde·
lifes laðð̄eow· leohtes wealdend·
asundrod fram sinnum· swa þin sunu mære·
þurh clæne gecynd· cyninc ofer ealle·
12 beald gebletsod· boca lareow

heah hige frofer·¹

Sicuta ert in principio.

Swa wæs on fruman· frea mancynnes·

ealre worlde· wlite & frófer·²
16 clæne & cræftig· ð̄u gecyddest ꝥ·
þa ð̄u éce god ána geworhtest
þurh halige miht· heofonas & eorðan·
eardas· & uplyft· and ealle þinc
20 þu settest on foldan swiðe fela cynna·
and to syndrodest hig· siðð̄an on manega
þu geworhtest· éce god ealle gesceafta·
on six dagum seofoð̄an þu gerestest·
24 þa wæs geforð̄od þin fægere weorc·
& þu sunnan dæg silf halgodest·
& þu mærsodest hine manegum to helpe·

POETIC PARAPHRASE OF THE DOXOLOGY.

Gloria.

Let there be to thee glory and praise wide spread Glory be
Over all people, thanks and joy,
Might and mercies, and love of all the soul,
4 Peace of the faithful, and thine own majesty,
The world made beautiful. As thou canst sway
All earth's power and the air above,
Wind and clouds thou swayest all aright.

Patri et Filio et Spiritui Sancto.

8 Thou art Father of consolations and guardian of life, to the Father, and to the Son, and to the Holy Ghost.
Life's leader, the swayer of light
Severed from sins, as [is] thy glorious Son
Through pure nature, king over all,
12 Strong, blessed, the inspirer of books,
The high consolation of the soul.

Sicuta ert in principio.

As was in the beginning the lord of mankind As it was in the beginning,
Of all the world brightness and comfort
16 Pure and wise : Thou revealedst that
When thou, eternal God, alone wroughtest
Through thy holy might, heavens and earth,
Countries and air above and all things.
20 Thou settest on earth very many kindreds,
And severest them afterwards abroad.
Thou formedst, eternal God, all creatures
In six days: on the seventh thou didst rest,
24 Then was complete thy fair work,
And thou thyself hallowedst Sunday,
And madest it glorious for a help to many ;

þone heaan dæg healdað & friðiað·

28 ealle þa ðe cunnon· cristene þeawas
haligne heortlufan· & þæs hihstan gebod·
on drihtenes naman· se dæg is gewurðod·

Et nunc et semper.

And nu symle þine soðan weorc
32 & þin micele miht manegum swutelað·
swa þine cræftas híg cyðað wide·
ofer ealle world ece standað·
godes hand geweorc groweð swa þu hete·
36 ealle þe heriað· halige dreamas·
clænre stæfne· & cristene bec
eal middan eard· & we men cweðað·
on grunde her· gode lof & þánc·
40 éce willa & þin agen dom·

Et in secula seculorum.

And on worlda world· wunað & rixað·
cyninc innan wuldre· & his þa gecorenan·
heah þrymnesse· halige gastas·
44 wlitige englas & wuldor gife·
soðe sibbe· sawla þancung·
modes mildse· þar is seo mæste lufu
haligdomes heofonas syndon
48 þurh þine écan word æghwær fulle·
swa synd þine mihta ofer middan eard·
swutole & gesýne þæt þu hig silf worhtest·

Amen.

We ꝥ soðlice secgað ealle
52 þurh clæne gecynd· þu eart cyninc on riht·
clæne & cræftig· þu gecyddest ꝥ·
þa ðu mihtig god man geworhtest·
& him on dydest orð and sawle·
56 sealdest word & gewitt · & wæstma gecynd·
cyddest ðine cræftas· swilc is cristes miht·

That high day all will hold and observe
28 Who understand Christian customs,
Holy love of heart, and the commands of the Highest,
In the Lord's name the day is honoured.

Et nunc et semper.

And now ever thy true works
32 And thy great might is manifest to many,
As they make known abroad thy wisdom
They stand eternal over all the world,
God's handy work grows as thou didst command,
36 All praise thee, the holy choruses
With pure voice, and Christian books,
All the earth; and we men say
Here on earth, "Be praise and thanks to God
40 Eternal joy, and thine own majesty."

is now and ever shall be,

Et in secula seculorum.

And for ever and ever he dwells and reigns
King in glory, his chosen ones
In high majesty, holy spirits,
44 Glorious angels, and mighty powers,
Faithful peace, thankfulness of souls,
Kindness of heart. There is the highest
Love of holiness. The heavens are
48 Through thine eternal word everywhere full:
So is thy might over the earth
Clear and visible as thou thyself wroughtest them.

world without end.

Amen.

We all say the Amen.
52 Through pure nature thou art rightly king,
Pure and wise, thou revealedst that
When thou, mighty God, createdst man,
And into him didst put breath and soul,
56 Gavest him speech and wisdom, and nature of increase,
Thou revealedst to him thy knowledge. Such is Christ's might.

Amen.

NOTES.

OF DOOMSDAY.

Line 2.—*beþeht*. The better orthography would be *beþeaht*, but it is not unusual for verbs whose stem ends in *cc* to drop the second vowel in the participle. Cf. *gedreccan*, Nic. 6 : "*þæt he hæfð on slæpe þin wif gedreht*." See also March, A.S. Gram. p. 111.

Line 2.—*holte tomiddes*. The same collocation is found in Alfred's Metres, 13, 38. It may be useful to observe such similarity of phraseology, with the object of fixing the date of this poem.

Line 4.—*gehæge*. This word is not given by Bosworth or Grein; the former has the simple form *hege*. The oldest form of the nominative was probably *gehæga*.

Line 5.—*wynwyrta*. Though *wyn* is of common occurrence compounded thus, yet this word seems unique. But *wynburg*, *wynmæg*, and other like compounds, are found in plenty.

Line 6.—*innon*. The unsettled orthography is seen by comparing this form with that in line 1, which is the earlier form. The rime is also to be noticed in the two sections of this line. *Amid the gathering* (*i.e.* of other plants).

Line 8.—*gryre*, properly *horror*; but of the inanimate *wolcn* horror can scarcely be predicated, and therefore the word seems rather to indicate the terrific character or roaring of the wind, and thus almost to be equal to a descriptive adjective.

Line 8.—*gehrered*, perhaps better=agitated, coming from *hreran*, rather than *hreosan*; but see Bosw. 28u. The more usual word is *onhrered*. See Grein, s.v.

Line 11.—*onhefde mid sange*=Germ. *hub an zu singen*. *fers* not given in Grein, and only cited as occurring in a grammar and dictionary by Bosworth.

Line 12.—*gemunde*, an adjective=*gemynde* for *gemyndig*. It occurs in Elene, 1064.

Line 13.—*tid.* *gemyndgian* is constructed with both accusative and genitive.

Line 15.—*Ic ondræde me eac*, I also feared. The corresponding verb is reflexive in German too.

Line 22.—*þara haligra.* *haligra* is here the substantive. Cf. Ps. li. 8.

Line 23.—I have written *yfel* rather than *yfeles*, because of the case of *witu.*

Line 25.—*murcnigende*, the word occurs in St. John vii. 33.

Line 27.—*ontynan*, conj. for *ontynen.* This variation is not uncommon. See March, p. 86. Thus we have the classic form *hæbben* in Guthlac (Exon), 644; *habban* in Ps. lxxxv. 16, and *habbon* in Ps. cxxi. 8, each for the present conjunctive.

Line 28.—*hate*, the adverb.

Line 30.—*Breost* must be the acc. plur., as the adjective shows.

Line 30.—*gebedstowe*, one word, though written *divisim* in the MS., cf. Juliana, 376.

Line 32.—*gearnade*, i.e. *ge-earnade.* This past participle is used almost adverbially in the sense of *deservedly.*

Line 34.—*wandian*, like *ontynan*, 27.

Line 42.—*breostes*, etc. These genitives depend on *gylt* understood from the previous clause.

Line 43.—*hæl*, cf. Germ. *heil*=safety.

Line 47.—In altering the MS. in this line, all that has been attempted is to keep as near to the written text as possible while giving a reading which can be construed. It seems most likely that the first *god* had been twice written by some scribe, and that the *i* of *mid* was then altered so as to make an adjective *mod-god* out of the two syllables, after the analogy of *mod-ful*, *mod-þwær*, etc. The Latin text helps but little, being *qui solet allisos sanare. Aglidene* is hopelessly corrupt, but as many of the letters of the word as possible have been preserved. It is thus left to the ingenuity of scholars, the exact letters of the MS. being given in the margin.

Line 49.—*nele*, a more usual form is *nelle*; *nyle* also occurs.

Line 49.—*brysan*, not in Grein, and only given by Bosworth on the authority of Somner without a reference.

Line 50.—*gemod*, apparently the same as *mod*, though I have not been able to find an instance of it. But the analogy of *hygd* and *gehygd*, and similar duplicates, is warrant enough for the meaning.

Line 52.—*gedwæscan* is not found elsewhere, but the simple verb *dwæscan* and the compound *todwæscan* occur. The writer of this poem was fond of *ge* as a prefix, v. lines 4, 8.

Line 53.—*gesceop*, properly the verb signifies *to shape*, hence *to inform*, *instruct*, *warn*. This metaphorical use is not common.

Line 55.—*forstent=forstandeð*. The successive changes seem to have been *forstandð*, *forstantð*, *forstent*, the last form also appearing as *forstynt*. The first words of the next line are *ſeo soðe hreow*.

Line 57.—*sceaða* is written four lines above *scaþa*. Both forms are equally common.

Line 60.—*be-bead=*bade, *i.e.* offered, as in the old expression *bidding of beads* for *offering up prayers*.

Line 61.—*lyt* is used generally followed by a genitive, as *lyt manna* =parum virorum, *lyt freonda*=parum amicorum. Here we have a construction wherein *lyt* seems treated as conjoined with *wordum*, forming a true compound, and therefore having the instrumental case at the end of the whole, after the analogy of such a form as *last-word* =fame after death.

Line 63.—*þa ænlican geatu*, for this construction of the accusative to mark the *way* after *faran*, cf. *For flodwegas*, Riddles (Exon), 37, 9.

Line 68.—*gearugne*. This form, which occurs again in line 91, is not the usual form of the masculine acc. sing., but *gearone*. The original of *gearu* was no doubt *gearug*, cf. *suprà*, 12.

Line 69.—*atihtum*. The weak form *atiht* as the past participle of *ateon* marks a late period of the language, the classic form being *atogen*. The former occurs, however, in Alfred's Boethius, 32, 1, Tit. 32. The tendency has developed in the later language, wherein we have *cleft* and *cloven*; *reft* and *riven*; *lost* and *forlor(e)n*, etc.

Line 73.—*scad*. Not found in this simple form; but as *gescad*, *gescead*, it is frequent enough. The like phrase to the text occurs in Matt. xii. 36 : *Gescead agyldan*.

Line 77.—*horwe*, a very rare word. See the Job in Thwaites Heptateuch, p. 161. It occurs below, line 156.

Line 77.—*afylled*, constructed both with a genitive and (as here) a dative.

Line 79.—*gyte*, a flood: still preserved in the Northern form *goit* or *goyt*, used for the overflow of a milldam, and the channel along which such overflow is conducted.

Line 80.—*beþunga*. The only form in which the nominative is recorded is *beþing*, but the interchange of *i* and *u* in this termination is very common, cf. *wearnung* and *wearning*.

Line 80.—*plaster* is a word of late introduction and rare occurrence.

Line 82.—*greotan* : the usual word in Lowland Scotch for shedding tears still is *to greet*. Here is another riming line.

Line 83.—*þa hwile*, the accusative case used adverbially. The more common form is *þa hwile þe*, followed, as here, by the conjunctive in expressions of indefinite time.

Line 84.—*Nu is halwende*, i.e. *Nu hit is halwende*. The complete expression occurs in Ps. cxviii. 103.

Line 86.—*gnorn þrowast*. The phrase occurs in Beow. 2658.

Line 89.—*men=menn=männ*. Dative singular.

Line 90.—*forhyccan*, i.e. *forhycgan*, the *c* having assimilated the *g* to itself, a very irregular form, for *cc* generally represents a previous *cc*, and *cg=gg* a previous *gi*.

Line 90.—*heaf and wopas*. The combination is common, but the form is more frequently *wop and heaf*.

Line 95.—*heah-þrymme*. Perhaps this ought to be *heah-þrymmes*, but as it stands it is capable of the rendering given to it in the translation.

Line 97.—*forebeacn*. For this plural form compare Grein, Bibl. Ps. cxxxiv. 9.

Line 99.—The alliteration in this line and the next is imperfect, and I am not sure that they should not be written all in one.

Line 101.—*Beorghlið*, as a compound, occurs, see Grein, but the genitive plural *beorga* is much more frequently used of *graves*, and so the sense seems to be, *the doors* (*hlið*=lid) *of the graves*, rather than the meaning of the compound =*hill slopes*, to which the verbs would not so well apply.

Line 102.—The correction here is not needed. The genitive of *sæ* is sometimes *sǽ* (f.), sometimes *sæs* (m.).

Line 104.—*bið*. This word has been translated here and elsewhere *is*, but in many places *will be*, according as the sense seemed to require. The Saxon having no future was compelled to use this tense for both present and future, and perhaps it may most strictly be termed a sort of aorist. No doubt to this circumstance is due the indefinite character of the modern English present, which may mean an act just in progress, as, *I eat=I am eating*; but in such a sentence as *I eat salt with my potatoes*, has that aorist character which includes past, present, and future all in one. For instances of *bið* used necessarily as a present, see Morris, Blickling Homilies, part i. p. 17. Of him who knows not the brightness of the eternal light, it is said, *se bið blind*. On page 19, speaking of God, the writer says *he bið á wesende* =He is ever living. Yet in the very same sentence *& á biþ ece*, the word may be (as Dr. Morris renders it) translated by our English *shall be*.

Line 105.—*gewuxsað*. If this emendation be correct (and the difference between the þ and the Saxon form of *w* is so slight as to be easily confused), the word is for the more usual form *geweaxeð*.

Line 106.—*dim hiw*. I have not varied the text here, though we probably should read *hiwe* as a dative. after the adjective. But the words may be intended to make one compound adjective of the form *bærfot, mildheort, eaðmod*. This being possible, I have allowed them to stand.

Line 107.—Then the stars fall from their stede (or place).

Line 110.—*flecgan*. This is the reading of the MS. The correct orthography would be *flegan* (or *flygan*), a derivative from *fleogan*, as *began* from *beogan*. See Loth, *Etym. Engl. Grammatik*, p. 226.

Line 112.—Literally = *mortem indicantes*, and might = angels of death.

Line 113.—*eored-heapas*. I have not found this compound elsewhere, though similar compounds with *eored* are in use, as *eored-ciest, eored-þreat*, etc.

Line 113.—In the translation I have regarded *upplice* as an adverb, but I think it would be more forcible if taken as the adjective agreeing with *eored-heapas*, and the whole rendered *the legions of heaven*.

Line 114.—*stiþ-mægen*. This compound does not appear elsewhere, but is quite in accordance with other forms from *stið*.

Line 115.—For instances of *ecne* used thus alone as a title of God, see Grein, s.v. *Bihlænan* is the usual form of the verb here.

Line 117.—*sigel-beorht*. *Sigel* being used for the *sun*, and also for a gem or jewel, the compound is capable of a double interpretation. *Gem-bright* is Bosworth's rendering; *sun-bright*, Grein's. The latter seems more in accordance with Scriptural phraseology, cf. Rev. i. 16. The Latin text has *fulget sublimis in alto*.

Line 118.—*weorðian* is not recorded elsewhere as compounded with *be*, the compound form is *geworðian* in other places.

Line 120.—*æghwanum*, a later form, noticed by Bosworth, of the more classic and usual *æghwanon*.

Line 124.—*stent=standeð* (v. *suprá* 55). The form occurs in Alf. Metr. xx. 171. It has of course, though present, an idea of the future, which is made more vivid by the use of this tense.

Line 124.—*earh*, a later form for *earg*.

Line 125.—*amasod* and *amarod*. I can find no instance of the use of these words or of any verbs from which they may have come. *amarod* seems cognate with *amyrred*, the participle of *amyrran*, to distract, mar.

Line 127.—*surround*, i.e. they will surround. *ymtrymmaᵹ* for *ymb-* (or *ymbe-*) *trymmaᵹ*.

Line 128.—*aboden*. We should have expected the form to be *abeden*. See March, p. 100.

Line 139.—*þinga*, governed by *eal* in 136.

Line 141.—*ypte oᵹᵹe cyᵹde*, for the combination of the two verbs, cf. Bed. iv. 25, and iv. 27.

Line 143.—*alyfed*=concessum, yielded up, set open to every eye.

Line 144.—*Ufenan*, generally means *from above*, and there is not a parallel to the phrase in the text, yet there can be little doubt that *ufenan eall þis* is meant to represent the *insuper* of the Latin. The same words occur again, lines 212 and 221, to represent the same Latin of lines 106 and 138.

Line 145.—*lyft*. As the Lowland Scotch has the same word still for *heaven*, it has been retained in the translation, though not an usual word in English. It seems a pity not to familiarize as much as may be such relics of the old tongue in whatever dialect they may be found, when no attempt is being made to translate into classical English.

Line 146.—*foresteal*. Grein does not give the word, and the orthography in Bosworth¯is *forstal*, though no instance is given of the occurrence of the word.

Line 147.—*miht*. The more usual form of the instrumental case is *mihte* (see Grein), but *miht* occurs in Cædmon, Exod. ix.: "soᵹfæst cyning mid his sylfes miht gewyrᵹode."

Line 147.—For *forwyrnan*, see Bosworth, s.v.

Line 148.—On this line a friend has suggested to me that the reading of the MS. *eah-gemearces*, may be a compound form, after the analogy of *eagþyrl, eagdura*, and mean *eye-boundary, horizon*. Had this occurred to me, I should not have suggested any other reading, feeling bound, in every case where it is possible, to render the text, rather than correct it. The like change of *g* to *h* has been instanced above, line 124. The Latin text seems to mean *the limitless expanse of air*.

Line 149.—*under roderes ryne*, the expression occurs in Elene, 795.

Line 150.—*emnes*. The usual adverb is *emne*, and the form in the text is found as a noun elsewhere.

Line 152.—*read and reaᵹe*. The latter of these words is for *reᵹe*, as it is written in 165. The same collocation in the *Bi Manna Wyrdum* of the Exeter MS., line 46; in Grein's Bibliothek, p. 208, *read reᵹe gled*.

Line 152.—*ræsct*, written *ræscet* (165), from *ræscetan*. See Loth, p. 240.

Line 152.—The more usual form of *efesteð* is *efsteð*.

Line 154.—*brynæ*, i.e. *bryne*.

Line 156.—*afeormad* and *aclænsad*, for the more usual forms in *od*.

Line 158.—*folca unrim*, cf. Germ. *unzahl Leute*.

Line 160.—The adjective *forht* most frequently signifies *timid, terrified*; but in the Hymns in Grein's Bibliothek, x. 56, *on þa forhtan tid*=at that terrible time, and so the adverb in the text may be rendered *terribly* or *fiercely*. The other sense, *in their terror*, would be intelligible, but scarcely seems so apt. The Latin gives no word.

Line 166.—*bærnð* for *beornð*. For an example of this tendency compare also the English *learn* from *leornian*.

Line 167.—*heora heortan . . . syn scyldigra*. For the construction compare Goodwin's Life of St. Guthlac, 22 : *wæs sum his scipes-man þæs foresprecenan Aðelbaldes*. There was one his boatman (viz.) tho afore-mentioned Athelbald's.

Line 167.—*horxlice* for *horsclice*. An early example of the tendency which at the present day vulgarizes *ask* into *ax*, though curiously enough the original *acsian* had previously suffered metathesis to come into the modern *ask*.

Line 169.—*æniman* would be better written *divisim, æni man*. The *g* of *ænig* disappeared, but it did not on that account form a compound with the following noun, though here written so.

Line 169.—*arnum*. The adjective *aren*=honourable, meritorious, does not occur elsewhere, but it is regularly formed from *ar*, as *fyren* from *fyr*. The syncopation of the dative plural is like *fyrnum teagum*. Grein, Cr. 733, and Panth. 60, and *gefæstnode fyrnum clommum*, Andreas, 1380. Thus, *be arnum gewyrhtum = meritis* of the Latin text.

Line 170.—*gehende* (prep.) is constructed with a dative case. The earlier expression was *at handum*.

Line 171.—*yrnð* by syncope for *yrneð*.

Line 171.—The construction is *þurh ealle breost-gehyda*. *Breost-gehyda* being the genitive plural governed by *ealle*, which is in the accusative after *þurh*. *Gehyda* for *gehygda*. Grein gives one instance of this orthography from Cædmon, Dan. 732.

Line 173.—*stænt*, written *stent* in line 124, another instance of the fondness of the scribe for the vowel *æ*. Cf. *suprà*, line 154.

Line 173.—*astifad*, cf. *suprà*, line 156.

Line 175.—*hwæt dreogest þu*, cf. Grein, Juliana, line 247.

Line 176.—*gewepan*, only the simple form *wepan* is given in Bosworth and Grein.

Line 177.—Thou servest thyself, *i.e.* thine own pleasure.

Line 178.—*glæd*, adjective used adverbially.

Line 178.—*leofian* is not nearly so common as *libban*.

Line 178.—*galnes* or *galnys*, an unusual word, not in Grein, but given by Bosworth as occurring in the Cottonian copy of Ælfric's glossary.

Line 179.—Perhaps *þær* is an error for *þæm*, in which case the sense would be, "thou urgest thyself to that luxury."

Line 179.—*gælsa* is almost as unusual a word as *galnes*. But it occurs below, line 237.

Line 180.—*Forhtas* for *forhtast*. But it has been allowed to stand, because in the later language the second personal pronoun coming after its verb was attached to it, and the last letter of the verb elided, so *forhtasþu* may be intentional. Cf. Chaucer's frequent *seystow* and *artow*. But it may only be a clerical error, and no indication of the later usage.

Line 180.—*fyrene* for *fyrenne*, masculine accusative singular.

Line 181.—Here we have either a corrupt passage or the construction is most puzzling. *ondræd* is the imperative, and the sentence is =*ondræd þu þe sylfum*, i.e. dread thou for thyself. The writer seems to have considered the preceding interrogation equal to an imperative sentence, "Wilt thou not fear," equivalent to "Be thou afraid," and then to have followed it up by a direct imperative. For such an indicative (though not interrogative) sentence used for an imperative, cf. Ps. cxviii. 31 : *ne wylt þu me gescyndan*=do not confound me.

Line 181.—For *ondræd*, cf. Grein, Elene, 81 : *Ne ondræd þu þe*. But the passage is full of difficulty.

Line 183.—*weana*. It may be that this is to be taken as of the evils done by the tormented, than of the evils done to them. Then the rendering would be, "wages for evil doings." Bosworth quotes Bede (ed. Smith), p. 599, for this sense, which will suit this passage quite as well as that given in the translation.

Line 189.—*susle*, rather *torture, torment*, than with Bosworth's *brimstone*. The line is designed as a description of the *depth* mentioned in the line preceding, which depth existed in hell from of old amid fierce torments.

Line 190.—*synt*. The forms of this plural of the present indicative of the substantive verb are (1) syndon, (2) synd, (3) synt. The second occurs below (217, 285), and in Lár, 19.

Line 191.—*þrece*. This nominative form does not occur. Bosworth gives *þrec*. The genitive plural *gicela* cannot be literally translated.

Line 193.—*ungemetum*. This dative plural used adverbially is of frequent occurrence in the Psalms in Grein's Bibliothek.

Line 195.—*gryrrað*. This verb is not found elsewhere, but there can be no doubt of its meaning from its connexion with *gryre*.

Line 196.—*þis atule gewrixl*. This case pendent (either accusative or nominative) is taken up by the adverb *þærinne*.

Line 200.—*stearc-heard*, probably intended as a compound adjective, cf. *widbrad*.

Line 201.—*na-wiht*, one word ; written *naht*, 206.

Line 203.—For similar omissions of the relative, which are not common, cf. Sax. Chr. 963 : *an munac, Brihtnoð wæs gehaten*, a monk (who) was called Brihtnoth. Also Gen. xxix. 29 : *sealde ane þeowene Bala hatte*, i.e. (who) was called Bala.

Line 207.—*unstenc* is not found elsewhere, but as the original signification of *stenc*, and of its derivative verb, was *fragrance, pleasant odour, unstenc* is a natural compound to signify the contrary thereof.

Line 208.—*welras*. This word, which is only used in the plural, is elsewhere spelt *weleras*.

Line 214.—*Forhwi* is a literal representation of the *cur* in the Latin text, but the translator does not seem to have known that *cur* might be rendered *because*, otherwise he would have written here *for þy*.

Line 214.—*fyrgende*, evidently intended to translate the present participle *luxurians*, must be from a verb *fyrgan*, of a kindred signification with the verbs *firenian* and *fyrenan*, but such verb does not occur elsewhere.

Line 218.—*sperca*: the orthography elsewhere is *spearca*.

Line 221.—For *wihte* used thus adverbially, see Grein, Cædmon, Dan. 146.

Line 225.—For ʒ we should have expected a repetition of *þær*.

Line 229.—*sauwle=sawle* for *sawla*, the usual form of the plural nominative. But *sawle* is found, *Christ and Satan*, 296.

Line 232.—*mid ealle*=Germ. *ganz und gar*. For instances see Alf. Metr. 17, 22 ; 18, 3 ; 19, 3.

Line 234.—*hleapað*, i.e. will leap away in flight.

Line 238.—*scyndan*. This, which is the slightest possible alteration of the MS., makes the verb an infinitive, and governed by *gewiteð* (236). But it might be altered and a simpler construction obtained by reading *scyndað*, the plural verb being justified by the expression *ælc gælsa.* A like construction with the infinitive *slincan* occurs in the next two lines.

Line 242.—*on ende.* Thus used as adverb in Grein, Ps. lviii. 12, lxxviii. 5.

Line 243.—*lað* may either be an adjective, as translated, or a noun =an object of loathing or offence.

Line 251.—*geþeon,* an unusual form of this word. For *þeowan* is very rare. The usual word is *þeowian.*

Line 253.—*þeostra,* i.q. *þeostru.*

Line 253.—*genipð.* This verb does not occur elsewhere, but its meaning is sufficiently evident from its noun.

Line 259.—*gebrasl* is not found, nor *brasl* ; but it is for *brastl,* which is the same as the more usual *brastlung.*

Line 261.—*tintrega,* another instance of this masculine nominative is given by Grein from *Christ and Satan,* 497. The more usual word is the neuter *tintreg.*

Line 265.—This line is without alliteration, though containing a rime.

Line 267.—*ricxað,* an intensified form, *ricsað* or *rixað* being usual.

Line 275.—*lifað=lyfð.* Third singular present indicative from *leofan.* The more usual verb is *lufian.*

Line 276.—*heah gehrineð.* This emendation seems to most nearly approach the Latin text, *collocat Altithrono.* *heofon-setle* must be dative, and *hean* could not be taken with it. Bosworth intimates that *gehrinan* is sometimes written *gerinan* (see 28u), but does not give an instance, and the *nn* of the MS. is easily accounted for.

Line 278.—*sylð* ; the usual forms are *seleð* and *syleð,* from the latter of which, by a syncopation of which the writer seems very fond, the form in the text is easily reached.

Line 287.—This verse is incomplete, some phrase having fallen out which represented *splendentia castra triumphis.*

Line 290.—*læt* for the more usual *lædeð.* The same part of the verb is spelt *let* in line 294.

Line 290.—Of the last word in this line, *drut,* I can offer no explanation, and have therefore written *brut,* which may have been written as a form of *bryd.* This is however very uncertain. Could *drut* be a contraction for *deorut* ?

Line 291.—*frowe,* evidently the German *frau,* though it is not found elsewhere in Saxon.

Line 299.—*her=*in the world of bliss.

Line 300.—For a similar omission of the relative, cf. 203. *þæm*

must here be singular, as is shown by the verb. *þam* in the next line
is plural first, and then singular.

Line 302.—*unbleoh*, a word not found elsewhere, seems to be
intended as the equivalent of the *incolumem* of the Latin. The sense
may perhaps be arrived at in this way: *bleoh* may, as the name of the
colour *blue*, have been applied, as the English word is now, to that
which is livid from approaching decay; and thus *unbleoh* would bear
the sense of *uncorrupted*. But with a word which only occurs here
much must be uncertain.

DE DIE JUDICII.

Page 22.—The Latin text is taken exactly from the edition of Bede
as printed in Migne's Bibliotheca. Patristica. It is there included
among the doubtful works of that Father, and as has been noticed in
the Preface, this Latin is also attributed to Alcuin. Either author
puts the composition at as early a date as the eighth century.

LÁR.

Page 28.—*Lár*. The title has been adopted from the text of this
short poem (line 32). It is evidently intended as a supplement to the
Doomsday poem, though no Latin of it is found.

Line 6.—*fílige*. This adjective seems to be formed from *ful*, after
the manner of *halig* from *hal*, and *sarig* from *sar*. It perhaps would
be more correctly written *fulige*. It is left as in the MS., being
neither in Grein nor Bosworth.

Line 7.—*oftost symle*. The same collocation occurs in the Juliana
of the Cod. Ex., line 20. See Grein, ii. 53.

Line 11.—*adwæscan*, properly used of extinguishing a flame, but
this same expression *synne adwæscan* occurs in *Christ and Satan*, 306.
See Grein, i. 137.

Line 11.—*fela*, like the Latin *multum*, is followed by a partitive
genitive.

Line 16.—*on gemang symle*, nearly equivalent to our *withal*.

Line 23.—If the text be correct, *wylle* is equivalent to *wylle þæt*. I
have no instance of such an omission of the accusative before the
infinitive in an interrogation. Perhaps we should read *nylle*, and
make the sentence declaratory=It will not please.

Line 24.—*mihtu* (i.e. *miht þu*). This coalescing of the pronoun with the verb is a sign of late date. Similar instances are *hafastu* (i.e. *hafast þu*), *Christ and Satan*, 64 (Gr. Bibl. i. p. 131); and *scealtu* (i.e. *scealt þu*), Andreas, 220 (Grein, ii. p. 15).

Line 27.—*forwinnan* seems used in the sense of *oferwinnan*, to overpower, and so eject from a possession. I have not found another instance of the word.

Line 27.—*wealth* as the translation of *welena* implies, of course, every kind of *weal*.

Line 28.—*ealninga*, a late form of the adverb.

Line 29.—*laðum to handa*. The phrase *to handa*, with a similar dative of the person, occurs in Cædmon's Genesis, 1463: *to handa halgum rince*; and *to frofre*, with the same construction, as it is in the next line, is found in the same poem, line 955: *him to frofre*. ·

Line 32.—*digolice*, literally *secretly*, seems to imply that this precept was some *arcanum*, some deep and efficacious esoteric teaching.

Line 53.—The adverbs are difficult to bring into any English rendering; *earfoðlice* seems to imply the trouble spent in bewailing sin ; *earhlice*, the dread arising from the thought of God's anger.

Line 58.—The sense appears to be, "Find out how thou mayest leave without having received injury from them these talents which have been entrusted to thee."

Line 63.—*hremi*, i.e. *hremig*. This is an instance of the stage through which most of our adjectives in *y* have passed: as *anig* into *any*, *sælig* into *silly*.

Line 66.—*þæt* is certainly pleonastic, and perhaps should be omitted.

ORATIO POETICA.

This prayer, together with the two paraphrases which follow it, have already been printed in Wanley's Catalogue, appended to Hickes's Thesaurus; but as they were evidently a portion of what precedes them in the MS., it has been deemed advisable to reprint them.

Line 1.—*Thænne*. This first word indicates a connexion between what is to come and what has gone before.

Line 1.—*N* (like the *M* or *N* in the Church Catechism) stands as the initial of the name of the person addressed, and this letter may be used as an abbreviation for *Nomen*. It will be seen from the margin of page 36 how very corrupt the Latin portion of this composition is.

In lines 3 and 4 the Latin half of the line has disappeared, and no attempt has been made in reprinting to supply the hiatus, which is merely indicated by the incompleteness of the lines as now arranged. Such other alterations as have been made in the Latin have only been made that the text might be intelligible. The mixture of English and Latin makes the composition of little value grammatically, when in some constructions an English adjective is joined with a Latin noun, the government of the Latin noun being indicated in one way, and that of the adjective in another, as is the case in line 10.

Line 17.—*gebyrd-boda*. A compound not found elsewhere, but regularly formed as *gebyrd-tid*, and *wil-boda*.

Line 21.—*fricolo*. Another ἅπαξ λεγόμενον. Grein, who quotes the word from Wanley, makes it a noun derived *friclan*, to desire, and hence used adverbially it bears the meaning assigned in the translation, "fervently," "eagerly." He also connects it with the adjective *free*, greedy. A somewhat similar use of an accusative to express the means, though it is not here with a verb, occurs in Cædmon, Gen. 117: Folde wæs þa gyt *græs* ungrene=Not verdant *with grass*; and nearer still in the same poem, line 812, we have unwered *wædo*, unclad in weeds (or clothing), where the instrumental accusative *wædo* is a parallel to *fricolo* in the text.

PARAPHRASE OF THE LORD'S PRAYER.

This text has been published by Grein in his Bibliothek, vol. ii. pp. 287–290, and had been previously produced by Ettmüller, Scôp. 231–234, both having copied it from Wanley. For completing the alliteration in defective lines, and now and then for improving it, Grein has adopted the suggestions of Ettmüller, as where he fills up line 6 with *cyning wuldres*, or, as in line 11, reads *engla* for *gasta* of the text. In the present reprint the text of the MS. has been faithfully represented in most cases in the body of the poem, a transfer of text to the margin having been only made where it was clearly needful to do so.

Line 10.—*ealla*. The alteration by Grein to *ealle* is probably correct (cf. line 12); but as this form *ealla* is found in Alfred's Metres, xx. 128 (Grein ii. 319), it is deemed best to leave it unchanged in this reprint.

Line 15.—*ræcað*. This is Ettmüller's correction, adopted by Grein, and absolutely necessary.

Line 18.—*heah nama.* Ettmüller would read as one word, but this is not needed.

Line 30.—*sib.* Ettmüller proposes *sibbe*, the more usual form, but these feminines of the strong declension have both forms of the accusative, some words using one form more than the other. Cf. *dæd*, in which the short form is the more usual. On the other hand, in nouns like *lufu*, the accusative in *e* is so much the more common, that *lufu* of the MS. has been transferred to the margin. This is the only example of *lufu* as accusative which Grein quotes.

Line 33.—*mannum to frofre*, cf. supra *Lár*, line 29.

Line 42.—*þinre. sinre* is probably correct, as Grein reads; but it is just possible to attach a meaning to the text of a subtle character, as implying that Son is one with the Father, and for this reason *þinre* is allowed to stand.

Line 43.—The neuter *gecynd* requires us to read *æþele*. The MS. has *þin*, not *þine*, as Wanley prints.

Line 47.—*fægere*, omitted in Wanley, and no suggestion made by Ettmüller or Grein. This reading of the MS. makes the line complete.

Line 55.—*ealre.* Wanley printed *ealra.* Grein suggests *ealre*, which the MS. has.

Line 66.—Grein and Ettmüller read *ælcre gecynde.* The text is very harsh, but may be rendered as an accusative=" But *as to each race* thou gavest [it] its peculiar habits."

Line 68.—*sænst*, i.e. *senst*, which Grein reads; but as the form *sændest* occurs in line 7, it is better to let this peculiarity of the orthography remain.

Line 70.—In this incomplete line Grein adopts Ettmüller's addition of *rumheort hlaford* to fill up. It will do as well as anything else, and occurs in line 63. Probably, therefore, it was not the text in this line.

Line 80.—Here Wanley has omitted *fæste*, which the MS. gives. Ettmüller suggested *frofre.*

Line 82.—Wanley printed *cyninge.* In MS. the last letter is *c.*

Line 86.—So here, too, the MS. has the correct *arisað*, which Wanley gave as *ariseð.*

Line 87.—*acænned*, i.e. *acenned*, but see note on line 68.

Line 88.—*eft*, omitted by Wanley. *gebrosnodon=gebrosnodan.*

Line 98.—*are*, thus in MS., Wanley *arc.*

Line 100.—*mihta* MS., Wanley *nihta.* Both these corrections had been made by Grein.

Line 111.—*gifnesse*, as suggested by Grein, though not introduced into his text, is probably correct, but see note on line 30.

Line 118.—*gecydd=gecyðed*. But in a poem so late as this we need not substitute the earlier form, though Grein has done so.

PARAPHRASE OF THE DOXOLOGY.

This poem has also been printed by Grein (vol. ii. pp. 291, 292), and likewise by Bouterwek and Ettmüller from Wanley, see Grein, ii. 411.

Line 13.—*higefrofer=higefrofor*. Grein adds to this line *and halig gast*, which completes the alliteration, but he does not say from whence he derives the addition.

Line 23.—After *dagum* Grein inserts *and on þone*, to make the sense complete, but the words can be understood without the addition.

Line 27.—*heaan=heán*. On this form see March, Ang.-Sax. Gr. page 61, compared with page 59.

Line 27.—*friðiað*. Here Grein adopts the more usual and classic form *freoð-iað*, but this is to give to poem a form which does not belong to it. The other form is found both simply and in composition.

Line 33.—Grein prefers *heo*, referring to *miht* in the previous line, but *hig* can be construed as referring to *weorc*.

Line 47.—Here Grein reads *halige domas*.

Line 49.—Grein shows some inconsistency in adopting *middangeard* as the reading here, but leaving *middaneard* in line 38. MS. and Wanley have *middaneard* in both cases.

INDEX VERBORUM.

The numbers which have no preceding letter refer to the lines of *Doomsday;* those preceded by L to the *Ldr;* those by O to the *Oratio Poetica;* those by P to the *Paraphrase of the Lord's Prayer;* those by D to the *Paraphrase of the Doxology.*

gelimpeð, 256
gelome, L. 31
gelyfð, L. 33
gemærsod, P. 44
gemang, 280, 282; L. 16
gemearces, 148
gemenged, 190
gemet, 224; L. 50
gemetað, P. 30
gemiltsað, O. 1
gemod, 50
gemonge, 6
gemunde, 12, 21, 24
gemyne, 92
genipð, 253
genipu, 110
geo, *adv.* 182
geond, D. 2; P. 26
geopeniað, 37
geopenod, P. 36
geopnod, D. 1
georne, L. 40
geotan, 82
gereordum, P. 19
gerestest, D. 23
gerinnað, 276
gesælig, 246
gesæligost, 247
gesælða, O. 6
gesceafta, P. 64
gcsceop, *pret.* 53
gesecan, L. 72
gesettest, P. 21
gesewen, 202
gesingod, P. 116
gesomnað, L. 41
gestigan, L. 2
gestryndes, L. 22
geswæccan, 206
geswenced, 255
gesweotolude, 134
geswinc, 256
gesworcen, 105
gesylle, L. 21
gesymed, 58
gesync, D. 50
gesyntum, 248

geteald, 133
geteode, 182
geþancas, 135; L. 52
geþencan, L. 77
geþeode, 282
geþeon, 251
geþohte, 136
geþwærnes, 270
geunne, O. 5
geweald, L. 35
geweorc, D. 35; P. 112
gewepan, 176
gewil, P. 78; L. 39
gewitad, 232
gewiteð, 235, 236
gewitnesse, P. 95
gewitt, D. *acc.* 56
gewlitegod, D. 5
geworden, P. 89
geworhte, 215
geworhtest, D. 17, 22, 54
geworhton, P. 91
gewrixl, 196
gewurðe, P. 35
gewurðod, D. 30; P. 59, 124
gewuxsað, 105
gewyrhta, P. 16
gicela, 191
gif, 86, 300; L. 2, 25, 38, 76
gifað, P. 103
gife, D. 44; L. 49
gifu, 279
gifnes (?), P. 111
gifnesse, P. 55, 115
glæd, 86, 178
glædlice, 272; L. 72
glengað, L. 12
gnagað, 211
gnorn, 86
gnornung, 266
god, 268
goda, 272
gode, 47
godes, 285, 290
godra, L. 12
greotan, 82
grimmum, 189

STEPHEN AUSTIN AND SONS, PRINTERS, HERTFORD.